He was kneeling beside her, holding her in his arms. She was still warm, but the life was gone from her body. Her open eyes were dull, and no longer full of the life and joy that seemed to inhabit them at all other times. She was gone, and he had to understand that. But what hurt most of all was the knowledge that it was his fault.

He began to convince himself that if he had arrived mere moments earlier, he could have prevented this tragedy, but he was too late and she was dead now.

The guilt that he felt for her death slowly transformed into anger. Rage built in the pit of his stomach, unlike anything that he had ever felt before. It was growing by the second and would consume anything in its path until it got what it wanted. Revenge. Plain and simple revenge. It was all he wanted and all he could think of until the monster responsible for her death lay just as lifelessly as she did now. Lifeless. Dead. Gone.

Chapter One

TJ quickly leapt away from the charging man. He had watched him enter the cave but that advantage was short-lived as they now shared the same suffocating darkness. Both knew that if they attempted to locate the other with their flashlight, they would expose their location before finding their foe.

TJ did, however, have another distinct advantage. He had been in the cave before and had selected it for a reason. TJ crept along the wall of the cave, listening to the waning footsteps of the other man. He then located and followed the cord towards the crevice. As he tried to squeeze into the crevice, the jagged cave wall ripped and tore through his clothes.

The noise caught the attention of the other man, and as he approached, his footsteps became audible once more. TJ reached to his side and grabbed the tripwire off of the cave wall and pulled. Nothing happened. TJ frantically pulled it again, but still nothing happened. The man was now dangerously close.

TJ attempted to shield his ears and eyes with his left arm as he gave one final, violent tug on the tripwire. The wire gave, and his hand flew back into the cave wall.

There was a flash of light and a violent thunderous roar that only intensified as it echoed throughout the cave.

With ringing ears and blinded eyes, TJ fell out of the crevice to his knees. As his hearing returned, he heard the shuffling of footsteps near the mouth of the cave. His eyes slowly adjusted enough to see flashlight beams dancing upon the cave walls.

TJ pushed himself up and approached the people.

"Not exactly according to plan but it'll work," TJ said.

He then looked down at his bloodied hand.

"Anyone have some bandages?"

"Yeah we got some." Roberts responded.

Roberts then handed him the bandages and, as TJ bandaged his hand, he began to relax. He had gotten the job done.

Chapter Two

TJ walked down the aisle, pushing the cart in front of him. He stopped, picked up a box of Cinnamon Toast Crunch, and tossed it into his cart. As he continued down the aisle his phone began to buzz. He pulled it out and looked at the caller ID. It was his mom.

"Hello," TJ answered.

"Hey, TJ I'm on break at work so I can't stay on the phone long, but I was on Facebook the other night. Do you remember that cute blonde girl that played soccer from high school? I think her name was Amy?

"Emy." TJ corrected her.

TJ remembered her, even though it had been five years since he last saw her. He knew Emy because she had played soccer and basketball for the high school. Even though she was a couple years younger than him she had a reputation among many of the guys as being one of the prettier girls the school had to offer. "Yeah, I remember her. Why?"

"Well I don't mean to intrude, but I saw that she just moved into your area. I think it'd be nice for you to reach out and try to reconnect with her."

"No, mom, it's fine. Thanks for telling me, I'll think about it."

"Love you, honey. Got to go."

"Love you too, Mom. Thanks." TJ hung up his phone, but instead of putting it back into his pocket, he scrolled to his contacts and found a phone number he hadn't texted or called in over a year.

Saturday afternoon TJ went through his closet, looking for something to wear. He wanted to make sure he was presentable, but he didn't want to over-do it. He wasn't sure what would be considered appropriate, so he decided he would err on the side of comfort. He put on a pair of jeans and a nice golf polo.

TJ pulled into the Italian restaurant ten minutes earlier than he and Emy had agreed to meet. He walked inside and looked around. He didn't recognize a person, but he didn't expect to. He rarely went out besides occasionally going to a sports bar to catch a Hawkeyes game. He thought back to the last time he had seen Emy. She was one of about fifteen people that had surprised him with a going away party before he left for basic training in the spring of 2011.

They had been friends, but most people had in the small school he came from. Their relationship was mainly limited to group events. He had driven home and pulled up to the curb in front of his house. His parents were outside washing their cars. TJ stepped out of his car, said hello to his parents, and walked up the driveway to punch in the numbers to the garage code.

It opened, but instead of an empty garage, TJ was greeted with a group of friends and the family pool table that they had moved from the house. One of his friends had brought an Xbox and television while someone else had brought beanbag chairs and a dartboard. The family's mini-fridge was stocked with soda and there were Domino's pizzas on a table.

He had arrived home at about 4:30, and it was close to 3:00 the next morning when people started to leave. They had talked, shared their favorite TJ stories, re-lived sports games they had been part of, stargazed, and had a Call of Duty tournament before it was over. They had given TJ a hard time because he didn't do well in the Call of Duty tournament and was still going to be a Marine. He smiled as those memories raced through his head.

"Sorry I'm late," Emy said.

TJ, startled by her voice, looked up and said, "Don't be, it's fine."

The two friends were escorted toward the back of the restaurant and seated in a small booth.

The waiter gave them their menus and left them to chat.

They spoke of their high school years, then about how their families had been doing before turning to more recent things.

As they spoke, Emy's phone beeped.

"I'm sorry," she said, "I thought I had the volume off."

TJ told her it was all right as she pulled out her phone and tapped the screen a few times before turning it off and putting it back into her purse.

"Sorry," she continued, "That project needed my response."

"Project?" TJ inquired.

"Yeah, my team needed my help. We're working on developing software for smartphones and tablets and stuff like that. We take a person's idea and turn it into something that works."

Emy knew he was a Marine, but had lost track of him, because she could no longer find him on Facebook. She didn't know what happened to him, if he had retired, or advanced. He had disappeared off the face of the earth as far as she was concerned.

After receiving their food Emy finally asked him, "So I haven't heard from you until recently, what have you been up to?"

TJ stuttered and stammered as he tried to answer, "I... I-I've just been overseas and all over the place." He struggled, "It's been kinda rough." As he said that Emy noticed his face become blank for a moment before he looked back at her. There was obvious pain in his eyes. Emy didn't know what to do, she just felt guilty for asking a question that would elicit that response.

She could tell by the way TJ shifted in his seat that it was a difficult position she had just put him in. It wasn't on purpose. She was interested in knowing more about what TJ had done while overseas. Now, as she looked at him, she knew it was a hard subject for him, so she stayed quiet, not wanting to risk stirring up such raw emotion.

TJ silently thought about how to move the conversation forward but he couldn't. His mind was fixated on his time overseas, it haunted him before and it was haunting him now. He endured the silence a moment longer before the waiter came around.

The waiter's words cut through the awkwardness that had settled in the air. "Would you like some more to drink?"

"Yeah." TJ thanked the man as he carried the cup away. TJ silently ate, nervously twirling noodles around his fork as he contemplated how to continue the conversation.

Emy couldn't help but to empathize with him. This wasn't the normal TJ, at least not the TJ that she remembered. He used to be confident and outgoing and even though she hadn't seen him for a few years, she was still surprised by how unlike himself he seemed.

As they begin to talk once again they went back to high school memories. Emy could tell TJ was more like himself, so she was content to stick with it. They spoke of how TJ had been injured in the third game of his senior season and missed a couple weeks with a dislocated shoulder, and how Emy had scored the winning goal her junior year for the state championship game in women's soccer. They laughed and enjoyed reminiscing and as their night was ending they made plans to meet again.

Emy knew that she would have to navigate their conversation with more finesse to avoid upsetting TJ, but she was also desperately curious to find out what had caused such a reaction.

They eventually began dating. They dated for several months. It was a testing time as TJ was redeployed. But he was able to return to her after an uneventful couple months helping support an operation in Afghanistan.

They grew closer as their dates became more intimate until TJ proposed to her. In March of 2016 they shared a small private ceremony, just the way TJ liked it. Family and close friends were invited.

They enjoyed a week long honeymoon in the Appalachian Mountains. TJ and Emy rented a secluded cabin and spent three days going out and enjoying the attractions offered in the surrounding towns. They went hiking for most of the fourth day and on the fifth and sixth day they relaxed in the cabin making good use of the hot-tub that was provided. But most importantly they enjoyed every moment they shared.

As they sat in their cabin they felt like anything they could ever need or want was right there.

Chapter Three

After three months of marriage TJ was tasked with going back overseas.

TJ didn't want to leave Emy, but he knew he must. It was what he did and what he was trained to do. Thankfully, no one that knew about Emy could connect him to his job.

When TJ got onto the plane, he could only think of Emy. The idea of having someone at home waiting for him was a foreign thought. It was weird how opposite his home and his job had become. He finally had something to look forward to that wasn't another mission.

Every day TJ dealt with the worst the world had to offer. Hate. Hate defined the world that TJ found himself thrust into anytime he went on a mission. But now, he had an escape from this. There was a woman waiting for him at home whom he loved and who loved him. Despite all the hate in the world there would be a small apartment defined by the love that the couple inside shared. It was an exciting thought.

TJ couldn't help but smile as these thoughts crossed his mind. It had been years since he had shared a home with anyone. He had moved away from his family after graduating high school and even though he loved them he was not able to go back to visit as often as he would like.

Just a few years ago during a mission, he didn't think any of this would be possible.

It was then, in August of 2014, that he thought his life was over. TJ shuddered at the thought of what had happened in that small Iraqi village. He wished he could shake those thoughts but, his mind kept wandering back.

TJ knew he needed to fall asleep but he was fearful of what might greet him when he did. He fixated his mind on sports as he began to drift to sleep, naively hoping that it would influence his dreams.

When TJ opened his eyes, he was shocked to see Emy walking in front of him. The sunlight behind her magnified her beauty. The light reflected off the fog that hovered over the ground. He stood and then sprinted towards her. It was easy to catch up because she had stopped at a tree line about thirty yards ahead. When he got to her he put his arm around her and pulled her close. He began to talk to her but she wasn't listening. Her focus lay elsewhere.

He noticed a look of sheer terror wash across her face as she stared toward the tree line. He examined the woods but couldn't see anything because the fog was so thick. His eyes continued to dart back and forth as he searched for this unseen threat. Finally, he saw some movement. A small glimmer of white that somehow stood out in the fog. It was shifting and moving through the woods. TJ couldn't figure out what it was. He had never seen anything like it. As the object approached, he eventually realized that it was exposed bone that he was seeing.

It was a skull, the skull of a deer connected to a rotting corpse with holes in it. The skull was completely exposed and the eye sockets seemed to stare at TJ. Once TJ's eyes met the gaze of the creature, it instinctively dove back behind the tree line and out of sight.

He knew he had to get Emy out of there. He grabbed her arms and tugged on her, but she didn't budge.

"Emy! Move! Snap out of it you need to move!"

It was almost as if she had looked into the eyes of Medusa. She was frozen solid. TJ yelled at her and tried to shake her out of her trance but to no avail.

Birds flew up from the forest. The creature had crept closer to them while TJ was focused on Emy. He turned to face it but when he did it darted behind the tree line.

He didn't have any time left. He squeezed Emy's arm and turned to face her. It was no longer Emy. TJ was now staring into the eye sockets of the creature. He screamed and jumped away.

His fear caused him to jump in his seat. TJ looked around but thankfully no one had seen him.

He slowly adjusted himself again to a comfortable position but he no longer wanted sleep. He wanted to calm down.

Knowing that he would remain awake and his mind would wander, TJ prepared to confront it. He didn't fight it this time but rather let the memory of what had happened wash over him.

It was a miserable Iraqi summer day, one-hundred and twenty degrees of fiery desert heat. TJ did as he had done many mornings, and left the Forward Operating Base to go on a run.

TJ exited and ran alongside the base before following a trail that led away from FOB Helen. He ran up a hill that eventually dipped into a valley hidden from the base. The trail continued across a creek bed and farther away. But TJ, as was his custom, turned and ran on the creek bed. Even though he knew that routine was dangerous he was convinced that no one would attack him there.

He continued running for a half mile before he saw a small boy lying down at the bottom of the hill. He was in obvious pain. TJ rushed to the boy's side to provide any medical attention that he needed.

"You're gonna be okay." TJ said. He knew the boy wouldn't be able to understand him but that wouldn't stop him from attempting to help. As TJ checked the boy for wounds he heard movement in the brush to his side.

TJ turned sideways in time to catch a rifle butt to his stomach. TJ gasped in pain. The attacker swung his gun at TJ's face, but this time, TJ had time to react. He ducked under the gun and used his momentum to propel an elbow into the man's abdomen.

As the man lurched in pain, TJ swung an uppercut into his jugular. As the man dropped to his knees unable to breathe, TJ grabbed the man's head and pulled it into his knee.

The hit broke the man's nose instantly. He fell onto his back still struggling to breathe while blood poured out of his nose. TJ turned around but the boy was gone. It had all been an elaborate trap. He needed to get out as quickly as possible.

TJ sprinted back towards the base. When he had made it twenty yards, gunfire erupted in front of him and bullets whizzed into the ground beside him.

TJ stopped to look up and saw a man holding an AK-47 coming out of the brush and approaching him. TJ had only one chance.

He feigned surrender by raising his hands in the air and slowly approached the man. They continued walking towards each other until they were seven feet away.

TJ then leaped to the side and charged at the man, tackling him into the ground. But as he tackled him a shot erupted from the gun and tore through part of TJ's calf. He writhed in pain. The man rolled on top of TJ and punched him in the face before hitting him in the stomach with the butt of his rifle. The man reared back once again and brought the whole force of his body down through the rifle butt into TJ's head. TJ couldn't defend himself and was knocked out instantly.

Chapter Four

When he awoke, TJ didn't know where he was. He blinked his eyes multiple times and attempted to roll off his back.

He felt rope holding him down. He tried to fight free only to feel an intense sharp pain in his back unlike anything he had felt before. He tried to focus on the pain in order to figure out what was happening. There were multiple metal spikes in his back, waiting for him to move so they could tear at his flesh.

He also noticed a small bit of softer material surrounding most of the prods. It was then that he had the horrifying realization that he was on top of a very old mattress. What he was feeling was the springs tearing through the covering and ripping into his skin.

He was stripped down to nothing. He struggled to free his hands and feet which were tied down. But as he fought his bindings he inadvertently drove the springs deeper into his back. He knew that the excruciating pain was exactly what his captors had wanted. The springs, like miniature meat hooks, ripped at the inside of his flesh.

As painful as it was, it didn't match the pain in his leg. The mattress springs poked into his open wound and tore at his exposed muscle creating, pain worse than anything TJ had ever experienced before.

He once again tried to loosen the bindings around his hands and feet but the movement only served to drive the springs deeper. TJ was certain that the springs had been sharpened for this purpose. Despair settled over TJ as he realized he would be unable to save himself.

TJ then attempted to divert his focus from the metal spears impaling his body. Instead he focused on his surroundings in an attempt to figure out where he was being held.

It was dark, even though there was a small lamp dimly burning on the other side of the room.

He guessed he had been unconscious for about an hour... two at the most. It would be difficult to carry a man too far from where he was knocked out at. That meant he couldn't be too far from the base. He hoped that someone would soon notice he hadn't returned from his run.

A few anguishing and disheartening hours later, TJ had given up hope completely. He realized, in his dazed state, he must have miscalculated how long he had been out.

He soon became aware of how truly alone he was in this darkness. There was no one he could call his enemy, nor anyone he could claim as an ally. It was just TJ all by himself, and it was a maddening thought.

Eventually TJ fell asleep but even while unconscious he could feel the spikes bearing into him. He awoke and felt a warm sensation on his leg. The darkness added to his paranoia as he tried to figure out what it was. A rat or a mouse was his original guess but soon another, much more fearful thought crossed his mind. Could the warmth he felt in his leg be the touch from the angel of death reaching out to him?

TJ's breathing became heavier and heavier. He tried, once more, to thrash his way out of the bindings. The only thing it accomplished was further slicing and tearing his flesh. As his body began to bleed once again he realized that his blood, not a rodent, or a supernatural harbinger of death was what he had felt.

After a few minutes of silence, a man with a light entered the room. TJ watched as this man approached until he stood over him. The light illuminated his face, revealing his identity as TJ's first attacker, the man whose nose was still obviously out of place.

The man kicked TJ in the ribs. TJ did his best to not gratify the man by showing him how much pain he was in, but the kick drove his body across the springs cutting into him even more. He lurched in agony but that only made it worse. He had accidentally worked the springs farther into his back. The man leaned over TJ, near enough that he could smell the man's breath. It was not a pleasant smell, and the treatment he had received from the man was even less pleasant.

TJ longed to be taken out of his misery, so he devised a plan to provoke the man into knocking him unconscious once more. As the man whispered threats into his face, TJ coiled his head back then head butted him in his already broken nose.

The man cried out in pain and let loose a trail of what TJ could only assume were profanities before kicking TJ four times in the face. TJ endured the first two, but the third knocked him out. He didn't feel the force from the fourth kick but he would feel its effects for a very long time.

TJ's eyes opened to the sound of a muffled explosion. He then heard gunfire. A man ran into the room towards TJ but another burst of gunfire sent that man sprawling onto the ground. TJ recognized him as the man with the broken nose. He was finally being rescued.

Chapter Five

The sudden jolt from his plane landing awoke TJ. He was back in Afghanistan, and he didn't know why or for how long he would be there. He picked up his bags as the plane stopped and minutes later he was in the desert heat walking towards the base. As he left the runway he saw a couple Marines standing by each other facing his direction. In their hands was a sign that read "Thomas Jefferson."

TJ chuckled to himself. He knew there would be someone waiting to guide him to where he would be staying, but he didn't expect to be welcomed like this.

He did, however, appreciate the humor some guys could find in any situation.

There was a time that TJ heard a man crack a joke in the face of almost certain death and it immediately affected the morale of everyone. TJ was convinced that that one well-timed joke had saved lives. He didn't understand how the man was able to make the joke but he sure glad he had.

It was obvious that the two men who were going to guide him were making their situation slightly better.

TJ approached the men, "Unless the third President was on the plane with me and I missed him I think you guys are waiting on me. Just call me TJ."

"Sure thing TJ." One of the Marines responded.

"So what's on the agenda today?" TJ asked.

"Well sir, we are actually in the dark in almost everything, we are going to take you to your barracks...er...uh your hotel."

The other Marine softly laughed. Calling it a hotel was wishful thinking at best. The honored guests of the base enjoyed full sized cots instead of twins and had small spaces to themselves, but that was it.

TJ knew that the set up would surely be scoffed at by most back in the States. But it was truly luxurious compared to other places he had been in along the way.

After arriving, he thanked the Marines who were waiting for him to put his bags down. They then led him to the command center. As they reached the entrance the Marines came to a halt, and saluted TJ. TJ thanked the men and walked into the command center.

He entered the tent and was welcomed by a young woman who seemed to recognize him before directing him to the back. TJ pushed his way past a flap and found Phillip.

Phillip had been part of the military longer than he had intended. He had planned to stay in long enough to retire, but he felt compelled to continue his career. He knew there were things to do, positions to take, and decisions to be made. Frankly, he didn't trust anyone else to handle those situations, so he never left, even though he wanted to.

Phillip put some papers down when he saw TJ.

"Welcome to the desert."

"I've been looking forward to a vacation." TJ responded with a smile.

Phillip chuckled, "Follow me, TJ, we'll get going."

TJ nodded then followed Phillip out of the tent and towards a running Humvee. They climbed into the back, and Phillip patted the driver's shoulder. Phillip then turned to TJ as the vehicle began to move and told him that he would share the details of what was happening when they arrived on location.

They drove for a while before finally pulling into a fueling station. TJ was surprised that there were so few people here.

TJ followed Phillip through the doors and back into a room filled with somber looking people. Phillip motioned for TJ to sit down before walking back into the main room. When

Phillip returned he wore a grave look on his face.

"Look, TJ, this isn't a conversation I want to have, but we need your help. We're being hit. We don't have a name or any physical traits. Our forces in this area are under attack and we aren't able to stop it.

"We are assuming it's the action of an individual instead of a group because no one has tried to claim responsibility for the attacks, and it would be easier for us to notice group movements. There have been quite a few IED bombings, PVC pipes with explosives stuffed inside them."

"Sounds like a normal IED," TJ interjected, "I don't get why you need me here for that."

"It isn't just a normal bomb," Phillip said with a dark expression, "There are a certain combination of chemicals that he puts in with the bombs," He sighed before continuing, "it's a nasty thing, white phosphorous."

"White phosphorous? You're serious?" Was all TJ could get out of his mouth. He knew that White Phosphorus would eat away at anything it touched, it would eat at a victim until it burned them to the bone, and as long as it had air to fuel it would keep going.

"Dead serious. That's why we brought you here; this is something that we need taken care of immediately."

"Okay, yeah, I'll get right on it."

Phillip gave TJ some papers with more information about the bombs and sent him back to the base. TJ entered his room and lay down on the bed. A chill came across his body. He knew the horror that white phosphorous could cause, and he had had too many experiences with IEDs.

In 2013, as a Marine, TJ and other friends in his squad were on patrol. They had walked near a wall before a blast sent them all flying to the ground while showering them with rocks and dirt.

TJ was in pain but he knew he wasn't badly injured. He rolled onto his stomach and pushed himself up to his feet. He turned and was shocked to find his friend, Sergeant Gregory Hall, lying face up covered in blood.

He rushed to him and was horrified to find Greg's left leg next to his body. His right leg was completely gone.

Part of his spinal cord was protruding from his abdomen. The heat from the bomb had fried his nerves and blood vessels. He wasn't losing much blood, but he was in shock.

TJ did his best to convince him he would be all right and that he would survive. But all Greg was able to do was force a smile and stare back at TJ as he passed from this life.

TJ was haunted by the image of what the bomb had done to Greg's body, but what was worse than that was the helplessness he felt as he looked at his friend and watched him die. TJ still had nightmares about that night.

TJ hated them and he hated the scum that made them. They were cowards, afraid to fight, but willing to kill anyone for their sick purposes.

His disdain for them grew as he read the details of what these bombs had caused. He knew the grief that good families had to go through because of them. Limbs ripped off, bodies torn apart, and fathers, brothers, sons, wives, and daughters, all lost in the blink of an eye.

That was why TJ needed to hunt down this coward. He hoped that the man would get what he deserved, an off-the books CIA interrogation site where he would be tortured for hours. That was what TJ really wanted, but first and most importantly he needed to capture the man.

He opened the packet and quickly noticed how little information there was. It was an aggravating process for TJ, and after an hour of looking over all the information he still didn't know anything. He pulled out a map and marked the location of the bombings in an attempt to guess at the bomber's base of operations.

It was crude, but with the general locations of the bombings marked he had a chance to narrow the area down. He knew he needed more info and a better feel for the area, so he studied the map for another fifteen minutes. He looked over the area where the fueling station was located and then went back over all the information he was given. Still there was not enough to help him.

He went to bed frustrated and disappointed that night. TJ didn't sleep well because his mind refused to stop focusing on the bombs. He tossed and turned, pondering the identity of this bomber, wishing he would be able to miraculously find him before anyone else died.

When TJ awoke, he grabbed a small breakfast and quickly headed towards the fueling station to gather more information.

He found Phillip working in one of the back rooms. He didn't want to interrupt, but he knew he wouldn't be able to get any of his work done without more information.

"Excuse me, sir, I have some questions about these earlier bombings."

Phillip's head popped up from his papers.

"What do ya need TJ?"

"I'd like to get a more precise location for where these bombs went off."

Phillip opened his mouth to respond but was quickly interrupted by a large explosion that shook the ground, followed by the sound of raining debris.

TJ and Phillip ran out of the room and found that the front wall to the station was gone. There were multiple fires outside, and the sickening smell of burning flesh filled the air.

Suddenly one of the trucks blew up sending, the men behind cover. A couple, seconds later, another was engulfed in flames. As the men scrambled to look for survivors, they heard cries and screams everywhere.

The others, who had been inside at the time of the explosion, attempted to stop the rampant flames from devouring anyone else.

TJ fell to his knees by a person who was rolling and screaming. He couldn't tell if it was a man or a woman because the soldier was seared so badly.

He attempted to quell the fire without getting burned himself, but it took too long. By the time that the flames had been put, out the person's entire body was burnt.

TJ froze, he took too long getting rid of the flames. Shocked, he continued staring down at the body until more screams shook him from his trance.

TJ was able to help the next person much quicker. She was lying on the road but the flames had jumped to her hair from her uniform. He cut off her uniform with his pocket knife and cut her hair before the flame could reach her head. Still a flame kindled on her arm. Without hesitation TJ took his knife and sliced deep into her forearm. He sawed off a chunk of skin and tossed it to the side where the flame ate away until there was nothing left. She writhed in pain, but she recognized that TJ had just saved her. TJ realized there was nothing else that he could do he turned to run back towards Phillip.

Phillip was walking away from another victim when TJ found him.

"I'll help out here. You run back into the station, jump on the sat phone, and get me a Medevac. Tell them we have thirty or so in critical condition, probably the same amount dead, and most likely a few missing. We will need extra security as well."

TJ turned, rushed back into the station and tore through every room until he finally found a working phone. He made the call and ensured that his voice stressed the urgency of the situation. He wasn't sure what they would need so he implored them to send everything they could spare. He hung up the phone after conveying the details, and then with a medevac on the way, TJ ran back out to Phillip.

"There is nothing we can do now except wait," Phillip said.

"There's got to be something more we can do," TJ said. "Do you think the bomber would have stayed around to watch?"

"I don't know, I wouldn't doubt it. But we have absolutely no resources we can use to hunt someone that may or may not be around."

"I'll go." TJ volunteered. "If he is in the vicinity I can try to find him."

After a bit of convincing, TJ was finally rushing away, searching for the one who had caused all this chaos. He carefully scanned his surroundings, making sure to recall what he had studied about the terrain.

Opposite of the station there was a large hillside. It would offer a great vantage point to watch the hysteria as it unfolded.

However, on the same side of the road as the station was a small, sandy knoll. It would offer a worse vantage point but a much easier escape into the valley behind it.

TJ had to make a snap decision, and he rushed across the road away from the flames and smoke and up the hillside. He was convinced that the sadist responsible for this was watching from up here. TJ was more determined than ever to catch him.

He made it to the top of the hill and continued along the ridge, examining the rocks and brush for any trace of the bomber but found none.

TJ saw that a helicopter was now landing and, he assumed it would pick up the wounded. A moment later, four more helicopters came into sight overhead, and deeper into the sky he could see an AC-130 gunship. TJ knew he had gotten his point across, and even though he didn't suspect a follow up attack he didn't want the station to be exposed to such a threat.

Chapter Six

By the time TJ retraced his steps back to the station the wounded were already loaded into the five helicopters.

"Any luck?" Phillip asked.

TJ shook his head and sighed.

As the adrenaline began to wear off TJ's senses were once again aware of the overwhelming smell of burnt flesh. It was only seconds after this sensation hit him, that TJ found himself on his hands and knees throwing up.

TJ had never been able to let things go easily. If something went wrong, he could have stopped it. There was always something more or something different he could do to stop it. He knew it wasn't healthy to always think like that, but he couldn't help it. The guilt helped to motivate him.

At the end of the day he was finally able to find a truck with room for him, so he hopped on and headed back to the base. He sat in the truck pondering what he should do next to track the bomber or pull him out of hiding.

When TJ arrived back to base he found the two Marines who had welcomed him upon his arrival waiting for him.

"Sir we were told to inform you to be at the command tent at 22:00. A few of us, will come by and get you about a half hour before then."

TJ thanked them and then walked over to his cot and collapsed onto it.

He decided that he would take a nap, not only to kill the time but also to get his composure back after the horrors of the day.

He had roughly three hours left before he would need to go to the meeting. With the troubles he had sleeping, he didn't think that waking up by then would be a problem for him. He would be able to sleep for an hour or two and then review his notes and be mentally and physically refreshed before the meeting. His eyes closed, but suddenly there was a metallic clicking to his left. TJ rolled out and off the bed, startled that someone had somehow entered without his knowledge.

As TJ slowly stood, he focused on the man who had entered the room. He was a large Arab who was holding an AK-47 in his hands. TJ tried to look at his surroundings for anything he could use but everything was a blur except for the man. TJ was then faced with the knowledge that if this man had somehow made it this far he surely wouldn't be alone. Even if he were to fight this man he would have more adversaries waiting for him outside.

"Okay TJ, let's go"

TJ froze, *"How does he know my name?"*

TJ recalled his previous kidnapping, he didn't want to go through that experience again and was determined that death was a much better alternative. If there were so many of them, there was no escape. The only thing TJ could do was fight.

The man stared at TJ, waiting for him to move. TJ slowly approached with his hands in the air. The man let down his guard by lowering the barrel of his gun away from TJ. He mumbled something TJ couldn't hear.

TJ knew now was the time to attack. TJ made it close enough to the man so he swung his elbow into the man's jaw. In the same motion he spun around and grabbed the barrel of the gun, angled it downward, then violently shoved the butt of the rifle back into the man's jaw. It was a hard connection and sent the man stumbling back in obvious pain.

TJ rushed him. The Arab saw TJ charging and kicked his foot out at TJ's legs. His foot connected with TJ's knee, dislocating it instantly.

TJ dropped to the floor in pain but as the Arab approached once more, TJ gave a final effort to stand and fight. He swung a wild left haymaker towards the man's jaw but he couldn't generate enough power.

The man easily blocked it before punching TJ twice in the abdomen. TJ lurched over from the pain, then the Arab connected with a haymaker of his own, sending TJ sprawling back onto the ground.

As TJ fell, his head hit the edge of the bed and searing pain shot throughout his body. TJ looked at the Arab who was now standing over him, his head was throbbing. His knee made his leg too weak to attempt to swipe the Arab to the floor. It was over. TJ had lost the battle and as he slowly lost consciousness he knew he would be prisoner once again, but this time there wasn't anyone that would be able to save him.

Chapter Seven

TJ regained consciousness and to his surprise his captors had made a mistake. He wasn't bound to the bed like he had been before. In fact, he wasn't tied up at all. He looked around and noticed he was in a tent occupied by only one other person whose back was to TJ.

TJ knew if he could somehow sneak up on him he could overpower him and could make it out of the tent. Then he could, at least, fight to the death. Anything was better than being held captive.

TJ silently swung his legs off of the bed, over the floor, and lowered his feet to the ground. He pushed himself off the bed and to his feet. As he tried to take a step, searing pain shot through his leg. His knee couldn't handle his weight, and he collapsed back onto the bed. He tried to pull his legs back and lay silently as if nothing had happened, but it didn't work.

The person quickly turned around, no doubt shocked by the amount of noise that TJ had just made. She was a nurse, and looked to be American. This was strange, TJ thought, *"Why would a nurse be working for them? Is* she a traitor?" As these thoughts raced through his mind she approached him.

"You okay? I heard some noise. You drop something?"

"What does it matter to you?" TJ shot back through clenched teeth.

"Excuse me?" she continued, "You are here, and you are my responsibility. Like it or not I'm in charge."

TJ had noticed the surprise on her face.

"Where am I?"

"What do you mean? You're still on base."

TJ slowly began to fill in the blanks and figure out what had happened. He stared at her blankly, unsure of what else there was to say. The nurse sensed his confusion and began to explain to him what was going on.

"You have a concussion, along with it some memory loss.

"A concussion? How?"

"You really don't remember anything do you?

"You and a Marine got into a fight. He got bloodied up pretty badly. Apparently you were knocked out. Thus the concussion."

"A fight?" TJ asked. "Over what?"

"I didn't bother to ask him."

TJ began to realize what had happened. There had been no Arab, but there had been an extremely vivid hallucination.

The fight was real, but for all the wrong reasons.

The nurse thought TJ was suffering memory loss caused by a concussion. That would excuse the incoherent babblings he had let out earlier.

It was really all working perfectly for TJ. He wouldn't have to explain a thing to anyone. It was comforting, but these feelings of comfort were soon taken over by feelings of guilt.

He was going to be forced to let that Marine take the fall for something that really wasn't his fault.

TJ knew the scrutiny would all be on the other man, which meant that TJ was going to be okay. The nurse brought TJ some medicine and a bottle of water. He thanked her, took the medicine, and downed the bottle of water.

He lay in bed a moment longer before sitting up and reaching down towards his knee.

He felt his dislocated kneecap and began to push on it and try to move it back into place. The pain was excruciating. As TJ moved his kneecap back into its position, he let out a scream. The nurse rushed back in to see what he was doing, but she knew better than to try and stop him in the middle of it. She cringed as she watched him finish.

He lay back with tears in his eyes. couldn't move his leg anymore because of the pain, but his kneecap was back in place meaning, that soon he would be able to walk.

The medicine he had taken earlier began to show its potency as TJ found himself extremely tired. He fought it like he always did but there was nothing he could do to stop it from happening. TJ fell asleep, but unlike too many other times, he slept peacefully. It was a deep, relaxing, and refreshing sleep. The first one he had had in a couple months. It was amazing.

TJ woke up an hour and a half later and stood to his feet. The pain was still there but it was bearable. He could walk, or at least hobble. He then found the nurse.

"Thanks for the help."

"You aren't cleared to leave yet."

"My knee is back where it needs to be so now I have to go back to where I need to be."

TJ circled his way through the base before finally making it into the command tent. He walked in and scanned the room for Phillip. TJ found Phillip in the back. He directed TJ to a couple chairs away from everyone.

"I heard what happened, are you okay?" Phillip asked.

"Yeah I'm fine"

"I don't care what happened between you two, you can't lose your cool like that. I need you here helping me, you can't be fighting our own guys like that when we still haven't found the bomber. Understood?"

"Yes, sir."

"We need a plan and we need it now. We cannot afford to get hit like we did today. Get whatever you need and do whatever you need to do, but make me a plan that will work."

"Yes, sir I'm on it."

"You better be. Now get out and get to it."

TJ stood up and walked away to leave the tent.

"TJ!"

TJ turned around and faced Phillip once more.

"Get some sleep. I need you at your best."

"Will do."

TJ nodded then walked out of the command tent into the cool crisp night.

Chapter Eight

TJ paced by his bed hoping that the pain in his leg would subside. It was working. He was able to walk, and the pain lessened with each step he took. Whether that was caused by the medicine he had taken earlier or if he was now able to handle the pain, he didn't know.

However, he did know he was tired and needed sleep so he would have to go to bed sometime. He paced for a couple more minutes, then crawled into bed. He rested his head against the pillow and finally let the wave of dreariness wash over his body.

He was running but didn't know why. He was surrounded by darkness and couldn't see a thing. He came to a halt and began to look around trying to find out what was going on. There was no light to be found. There was nothing he could identify. There was no moon or stars in the sky to provide guidance.

He began to run again, this time as hard as he could. As he moved, TJ became aware of the splashing sounds around him. TJ didn't know if he had just entered a creek or if he had been running in it for so long he had gotten used to it. The strangely warm water was up to his shins and was beginning to hinder his movement. He was running with the current. He could feel the current pulling his legs forward. The warm water finally came up to his waist and TJ knew that all the noise he was making would attract attention, so he slowed down and tried to let the current carry him.

TJ floated in silence for a few moments before a splash about thirty yards behind him shocked him into running again. It sounded like there was a group of people chasing him, and with the way they were gaining on him TJ guessed that they could somehow see him. As he pushed his way through the water he felt something brush against his leg. He continued past it but every few steps he felt the same sensation.

TJ thought there was something in the water swimming along the side of him or maybe he had felt something as simple as seaweed. He felt it again a couple feet farther as it wrapped around his leg. TJ was convinced that it had to be seaweed.

Another strand of seaweed wrapped itself around his ankle. But this time, it suddenly tightened and TJ tripped and fell into the warm water. He struggled to get his leg free as he tried to emerge but he gasped too early and the warm water poured into his mouth. As he thrashed to the surface, he coughed, spat and took in one last breath before he was pulled back under.

As TJ reached to free his leg, more of the seaweed caught his hands. He yanked and jerked to try to escape, but it wouldn't let go.

His lungs were burning from the lack of air. He couldn't hold his breath any longer. He lurched for the surface as he began to pass out, and the only thing he felt was water pouring into his mouth.

TJ was surprised by the sudden light. He stood up out of bed and took a couple of deep breaths as he tried to calm down from the dream. He was happy to be awake so he wouldn't have to deal with the horrors of his mind. Actually, he would be fine if he never had to sleep again. He sometimes felt as if he would rather die than sleep.

He put on a pair of shorts and shoes so he could go for a nice morning run. He didn't mind the cool crisp air outside because he knew it would warm up extremely fast. TJ stretched and was suddenly overtaken by the eerie feeling that someone was watching him. He looked around but saw no one.

He began to run and was pleasantly surprised by how well his knee was holding up. He was no longer hobbling or experiencing pain. TJ continued until he found a trail outside the base and followed it for a half mile before veering off towards a different path.

TJ didn't know where he was going, he just wanted to run. He was happy to be doing it, and was happy that, for a moment, at least, he didn't have anything to worry about. He was especially grateful for the nice breeze that was blowing this morning. Even when things warmed up, this breeze would keep him from being annoyed by the extreme heat.

He continued running and noticed that the trail became muddier the farther he went. To avoid the mud, TJ decided to run along the side of the path. As he stepped off the trail he tripped over a large rock that he didn't see. He stumbled and rolled down the hill until he came to a stop in a small pool of water.

He lay in the water, staring at the sky as he recovered from his fall. TJ noticed a putrid stench and then immediately sat up. He looked to his side and was horrified to see the body of a Marine whose blood was still trickling out.

He rushed and splashed his way over to the body, but the Marine was dead. His wounds were peculiar, but they weren't bullet holes, they were deep tears into his body.

TJ didn't know of anything that could produce that type of wound. An animal attack seemed unlikely, but the wounds didn't appear to be caused by a human. But what was even stranger than the man's wounds was that TJ recognized him.

TJ tried to remember where he had met this man. He wasn't one of the Marines that welcomed TJ to base, and he wasn't in the command tent when TJ had met Phillip. The only place TJ could think of where he might have seen him was at the fueling station. There were a lot of people there but he never got a good look at them.

Then suddenly, TJ recognized him. He was at the front of the fueling station before the bomb had gone off. TJ hadn't seen the man since. He wondered if it was possible that this man had somehow helped the bomber and escaped only to be killed by him later.

TJ knew it was unlikely, but he didn't think of any other reason that the man could have ended up out here. He reexamined the man's wounds, and blood was still flowing out. The blood mingled with the water, creating a very disturbing red pool.

TJ knew the next thing he needed to do was to go back to base and report what he had found. As TJ stood up he heard a noise come from the man causing TJ to cautiously back away.

He turned around to walk away, but when he did, he heard a splash behind him. He glanced over his shoulder, and the body was gone. He tried to run, but, in his panic, he fell forward into the pool of water. As he pushed himself up, he felt something grab his arm. He fought it off, but when he stood up, the thing wrapped around his leg. He looked to his leg to see what was holding him. It was the body. He kicked free of it and attempted to rush away.

Every time he took a step the pool seemed to grow larger and larger. He was running full speed, but he was making no progress.

He made another step forward and was grabbed again. He turned and struggled with the body until his other leg was seized and yanked back. TJ did the splits as he collapsed into the bloody water.

He attempted to break free and finally did. But after successfully fighting off the first body, there was a second corpse on top of him. He fought it off but soon found himself being attacked by many more.

He pushed past a few of them until he was able to run. He was then stopped in his tracks by a body standing in front of him. It was charred black and staring at him. TJ froze. There was nothing he could do and nowhere he could run. As TJ stared at this body, the realization hit him: all of these people were dead because he had failed to stop the bomber from striking again.

Chapter Nine

TJ decided against going for a run this morning. He rolled out of bed and tested his knee, and it felt good. He got onto the floor and began to do pushups, then rolled over, and did sit-ups.

He felt refreshed and ready to start the day. It was better than the nightmares that had haunted him the night before.

He sat down on his bed, pulled his notes out, and reexamined the little information that he had.

It was hard to focus because his mind kept thinking back to his dreams. Being there when the bomb went off was a horrific experience.

Not wanting to be discouraged, he left his room and went to get something for breakfast. He picked up a few granola bars and some water and walked back across the base to his room. He sat down and ate while looking over his notes.

He began to think about everything that had transpired since his arrival. Death and destruction, those two things seemed to be waiting for him.

He couldn't wait to get back home and to get away from it all. He had been gone for less than a week, but to him it felt like a few months. He missed his new wife and hated to be away from her. But even the thought of her couldn't lighten his mood. Any thought of her would be met by multiple thoughts about the bomber, his work, and the individuals that had been killed. He was soon interrupted by a sound outside.

TJ went to investigate and found three obviously distraught men. One was on his knees, crying loudly. As TJ approached, one of the others knelt beside the crying man.

TJ realized that the man who had just gotten onto his knees was a chaplain praying with the other. TJ knew that only one thing could make these men cry like this. Death. And the only deaths that had occurred were because of the bombings yesterday. He prepared to give condolences, but he knew he couldn't. He had nothing to offer, because it was his fault that they were there. It was his fault their friend had died. It was his fault that the bomber wasn't captured. TJ had no choice but to walk back to his room.

He sat down on his bed. He felt a burden of guilt because of these deaths and the way that it had affected these men. If he could have somehow figured out a way to stop the bombings, this wouldn't have happened.

TJ's mind was worn and the dreams he had been having made it even worse. The mental anguish and physical exhaustion had affected him in ways he didn't think possible. He felt desperate. He needed something to change, because he couldn't handle the guilt and sadness anymore. He couldn't handle the thought that he was at fault for the tragedy that took place the day before.

TJ began to sweat and shake thinking about what all he had seen. He could still smell the burning flesh. He could still see the faces of the people that were at the station yesterday. He could only remember two of his dreams, but the way his thoughts were affecting him was too much. There had to be a way to escape, TJ thought, and a way to get away from everything that was happening. The guilt that ate at him, the death that surrounded him, the nightmares that plagued him, all weighed heavily. He had to face the stark reality that the death of the bomber wouldn't bring an end to it; there would be something or someone to replace him. TJ needed to escape it all, for good.

Maybe there was a way that one death could stop all of the others from affecting him. With that thought in his mind, TJ leaned over, opened one of his bags, and pulled out a 9mm pistol. "*Yes, it was possible,*" he thought, one pull of the trigger, and he wouldn't have to deal with any more death. No more being haunted by his dreams. He could take care of everything with one shot.

He held the gun and looked into the barrel. It was a beautiful machine. If used in the right way it could save lives. If used in the wrong way, it could take innocent ones. But TJ wasn't innocent. His dreams reminded him of that. He raised the gun and placed the barrel of the weapon on his temple. He tried to regain his focus so he could do this one last thing.

His trembling became more violent as he placed his finger on the trigger. His hand shook and his body quivered. He slowly pushed the trigger as he took a deep breath to steady his hand. He finally pulled on the trigger but it didn't move. Nothing happened. He pulled again, but still nothing happened. Enraged, TJ yelled and threw the weapon to the ground. He was disgusted by the thought of it. The moment when he had needed his weapon the most it wouldn't work for him.

It took several minutes before TJ was able to calm down. As he sat on his bed, the realization hit of how close he had been to taking his own life. He was shocked that he had gone that far and was horrified by how easy it was. Soon he also realized that if it had worked he would have failed the people whom this bomber had hurt by not finishing the job and capturing him.

TJ was disgusted with himself. He leaned over and searched through his bag until he found a bottle of pills.

These were no ordinary pills. They were given to him by a friend of his. Tucker had studied psychology at Duke on an NROTC scholarship and had excelled in his schooling. He was among the top in his class at graduation. He quickly advanced through the ranks of the Navy but soon realized that he was still much more fascinated by the mind than anything else. For the past three years he had been in the Department of Defense, doing what he could to help improve the mental wellness of those who have served.

He was the man whom TJ had seen for a couple weeks after being captured and tortured. Tucker knew how important it was for TJ to get back to normal. He also knew that if TJ was openly suffering from PTSD that he would no longer be considered fit to do his job.

He tried to teach TJ to think and to act like a machine.

"Your job is to do as much as you can." He had said, "Not to question yourself afterwards. If you do that, it's a job well done."

After a few days of trying, Tucker was able to secure a small supply of anti-depressants formulated specifically to help deal with PTSD.

TJ swallowed two of the pills and walked over to pick up his pistol. As he inspected, it he was amazed to find that the safety was still on. That was the only thing that had stopped him from killing himself a few moments ago.

TJ put the gun away and sat down on the bed. He then picked up a pen and began to study the map.

The closest thing worth noting was Takht, a village approximately forty miles to the north. The base where TJ was currently located was strategically positioned just north of Zabul, Iran. There was nothing of importance in or around Zabul. But America, knowing that it would spread Iran thin, used her manpower to set up a base here. It also gave America another visible force to deter Iran from hostilities.

TJ studied the map some more. There were four bombing locations that he knew of, each of which he marked with a small dot. The farthest one away was between Takht and Darabad-ePa'in. The most recent one was the refueling station about fifteen miles west of Takht on the main highway. The other two were near Takht as well, one seventeen miles to the east and the other four miles to the northwest of that.

TJ figured that the most likely base of operations for the bomber would be in Takht.

The problem was that any sort of reconnaissance around the village would be extremely obvious. Even at a distance, they would risk being spotted. No, they couldn't track him down or hunt him. They needed a trap to lure him out.

TJ pondered all of the possibilities for this idea, then his thoughts began to gain traction. He left his room and hurried to the main operating tent. He entered and walked around but couldn't see Phillip anywhere.

He exited the tent, continuing his search for Phillip. He came upon a small group of Marines huddled around a small picnic table. The two in the middle were playing a game of chess while the others watched intently. TJ joined the group and watched the game for a moment before nudging the Marine standing next to him.

"Hey, do you happen to know anything about Takht?"

"Yeah, I practically live there these days." The man chuckled.

"Is there anything there at all that provides cover, or is it as open as it looks on the map?"

"There is a small ridge near the town, but it isn't much. Wait, last time we were there we walked the ridge. On the opposite side were some caves. We didn't go into them so I don't know if any of them open up or if they are too small for a person to get into. Besides that there isn't anything there."

"That actually might be just the thing that I need" TJ said before thanking the man for his help and walking back to the command tent.

He found the lady who had talked to him a couple days earlier. When he asked her where he could find Phillip, she pointed him to a phone and gave him a six digit number to dial. TJ picked up the phone and dialed the number, and only seconds later a man answered. TJ asked for Phillip. After identifying himself and stressing the urgency of the phone call, TJ finally reached Phillip.

TJ began to tell Phillip his thoughts and ideas about the bomber before laying out his plan.

After listening, Phillip said, "As of right now that's better than anything else we've been able to come up with. If it doesn't work it seems to hold very little risk to us, but if it does work we certainly gain a whole lot. Go ahead and do what you need to do to get this thing done. Do you have all of the supplies you need?"

"No, not yet. I'm going to need man power and equipment. It shouldn't be hard to find volunteers, and I am sure the equipment will come just as easily."

"Good. How soon can you get it done?"

"Within the next couple days, TJ responded.

"Okay then. I've got a guy you need to get in touch with. His name is Lance Roberts. Go find him and get to it."

As he lay on his bed that night, he thought about what he would need. Obviously, his first step would be to talk to Roberts and get his opinion on things and then run the finished product by Phillip once more.

When TJ fell asleep it was a restless sleep as every dream he had that night was of his plan backfiring and people dying.

Chapter Ten

TJ explained his full plan to Phillip and Staff Sergeant Roberts. TJ had already approached Roberts and convinced him that this plan could work, the look on Phillip's face, however, told TJ that he had yet to be sold on the idea.

"We can do this," TJ pleaded.

"My men won't have a problem with this, Sir. We are just waiting for the okay," Roberts said.

"Look, it isn't a question of whether it's a good plan or whether your men can do it. My concern is logistics. What resources are we going to be using and for how long."

"We won't know. But if we can pull him out there when we are waiting for him, isn't that better than him just showing up when we don't expect it?" TJ asked.

"Okay, I guess we don't really have a choice do we?" Phillip conceded. "Hurry up and get started."

TJ and Roberts walked away from the command tent, excited that they would get a chance to put this plan into action.

"So do you really think this will draw the bomber out?"

"Honestly," TJ said, "I'm not even sure if he is in Takht, but I think that it is worth a shot."

They continued walking until they found a small group of Marines playing football. When the men saw Roberts, they finished their play then approached him.

"Well, men, what's the score?" Roberts asked smiling.

"Uh, I think it is twenty-one to twenty-eight sir." One of the men responded.

"Okay, finish your game. Whoever hits thirty-five first wins, but if you come over here tired we are going to have some problems."

The men laughed and ran back to their field and continued to play. "It seems your men really look up to you." TJ said.

"Hypothetically." Roberts responded.

Roberts was a short man, as he stood around five foot eight, but was still very stocky. He was an extremely black man and TJ had noticed there was always some sort of hand or arm motion whenever he spoke.

TJ turned his attention back to the Marines playing football. Before long one team had the ball near the endzone. They ran a play action pass but the ball was overthrown slightly and a defender was able to catch it. The defenders momentum kept him going forward and he was able to run the interception back for a touchdown.

The men congratulated each other for a good game, then approached TJ and Roberts once more.

After explaining the plan, Roberts and the Marines headed back to their barracks.

TJ went back to his room and gathered a couple of his papers and his pistol and placed them beside his bed. He sat down on the bed and relaxed. He was careful, however, not to fall asleep.

After waiting for a few minutes, TJ picked up his things and walked to the trucks. Time passed slowly, and TJ was reduced to drawing in the dirt as he waited. His random drawings eventually turned to crude sketches of Takht, the road, and surrounding areas.

Roberts approached a few minutes later and joined TJ. "Hey, man, you ready to get this thing going?" Roberts asked.

"Yeah, I just want this to be over with; I'm ready to see if it works out."

"I sure hope it does, I don't want anyone around here to go through this again. You were at the station when the last bomb went off, weren't you?"

"Yeah, I was. It wasn't good. Some of those sights I can't get out of my head. There was one person, I don't... I couldn't tell if it was a guy or a girl because he was burned so badly."

TJ was overcome by emotion and it sounded more like a whimper.

"Oh, God, man, that's rough. I'm sorry." Roberts patted, TJ on the shoulder.

The rest of the Marines began to arrive.

In the waning moments before they left, the adrenaline and excitement became more obvious. The men were ready to go and when the drivers showed up they all piled in to the trucks.

It was dark out as TJ, along with Roberts and his Marines finally made it onto the road. It was around one in the morning when they made it to the location. There was no time to waste. All of the men jumped out of the trucks and grabbed all the equipment they could and set up camp.

By the time the sun peeked over the horizon the small American camp was complete.

A couple of the Marines led TJ to the caves that they had spoken of earlier and they took their time examining each one and its surroundings.

Roberts sent a couple groups out to provide security away from the camp. The camp was, by design, not hidden from the village. The hope was however that the villages would think it was meant to be.

Some of the villagers didn't care about the American presence; some wished they would leave so they could continue their lives in peace with family and friends. But there was one in Takht who became anxious at the sight of an American camp that morning.

Chapter Eleven

Dhul Fiqar knew that his time in Takht was limited. He noticed the American camp shortly after waking up. Even if the Americans weren't there for him, their presence would disrupt his operations enough to make him unable to continue his mission.

He needed the Americans out of the way. He rushed down the stairs to his workshop. He would need to take as many supplies with him as he could, but first, he needed to make one last bomb.

That was easy for him. He had made plenty of bombs. For this one, however, he couldn't wait for his white phosphorous. It would take too long to get the amount he needed. He would have to settle this time. He would make three bombs that all had the same detonator. He didn't even care about casualties, He wanted to send a message, and he needed to buy time. He would detonate the explosives as he left the village. By the time the Americans came around to cleaning things up, he would be gone.

The Marines at the camp had their weapons next to them in case of emergency. But most of them paid little attention to their rifles. They did, however, pay attention to their conversations, their poker games, and their bets on whether or not this plan would work. They knew the odds of being attacked soon after arriving were slim, so they tried to enjoy themselves as much as they could.

The only things they were asked to do were make sure that their presence was known and to be ready in case they needed to fight.

TJ and Roberts walked together to the caves TJ had visited earlier. Both men had flashlights out to illuminate the caves as they entered. The first cave had a small entrance that they had to duck into, but once inside, it opened up. The men walked along the edges of the cave and found that they were in the only room the cave had to offer. Even though it had opened up, it was still rather small.

The men crouched out and walked to the next cave. This cave's entrance was narrow and straight, but there was no need to contort one's body to enter. It, like the other cave, had a singular room slightly larger than the entrance. As the men walked along its walls, TJ found a small crease that ran parallel to the entrance. He squeezed into the crease positioning himself between the cave entranceway and the wall. TJ got out and turned to Roberts. "I like that"

"You do? Do you think we can make the rest of the cave work for ya?"

TJ looked around and walked along the wall that led away from the crack. The floor was rough but not slick. The wall had a few sharp edges, but not too many. "I think we can make this one work perfectly."

Roberts joined TJ along the cave wall, and then asked, "Where should we run the wire?"

TJ looked up. "Do you think we could get it along the ceiling?"

"Actually yes, that should work. If we run it from here," Roberts walked from the crevice TJ had just squeezed out of and towards the center of the cave, "We can place the flash bang over here."

Roberts walked towards the middle of the cave. Then paused, "Right here. This seems to be in the center of the cave. A blast from here would maximize the echoes and it would most likely blind him. The question is, can you handle it?"

"I'll have ear plugs in and make sure my eyes are closed." TJ laughed. The men walked out of the cave to grab the needed supplies to set their trap.

Chapter Twelve

Dhul Fiqar was not happy. He could see the American camp, but he didn't know when and where the Americans would be. Dhul knew it would take time to chart the movements of the Americans, but he also knew that time was not something he had much of.

He sat looking out of his window at the camp. His finger traced along the map of Takht he had made years earlier. He glanced at the map and the surrounding areas. The time passed slowly, and he made small markings on his map as he saw people move about the camp.

As the sun descended over the horizon, Dhul gave up on tracking the movements of the Americans for the night. But as he was about to walk away from the window, he saw a light moving behind the hills. He watched as another light, then one more pair of lights appeared.

They were headlights! Dhul had no idea why the Americans would be leaving so quickly, but he marked down the time then walked out of his house.

Dhul disappeared into the shadows. He swiftly made his way through the town and up onto one of the hills on Takht's side of the highway. He blended in with the surroundings as he watched the American camp. There was no movement, and that surprised him. He was shocked that they would completely abandon their post during the night.

He rushed back to his house and entered. He got into his bed knowing that tomorrow he would work on his bomb. He had changed his mind though and no longer wanted to make three separate bombs. Instead, he wanted to plant one and do as much damage as possible before escaping.

Chapter Thirteen

TJ and Roberts ate at the camp together the next morning. They didn't expect the bomber to show up in the first few days but they were still disappointed that he hadn't appeared. They conversed before continuing to check on the patrols and other aspects of the camp.

Dhul was at work before the sunrise that morning, but he did take a small break as the sun peeked over the horizon. He had always enjoyed nature and especially loved the sunrise. It was a sign of a new day, a new chance, new life.

He loved it, but he also knew that this would be the last one he would be able to enjoy in Takht, so he made sure to savor it.

Dhul worked furiously throughout the day. He was extremely meticulous in his handling of the equipment and ingredients.

As the evening approached he finally finished his work. He stepped back from the table and admired his creation. Even though he had finished it quickly, it was still well made.

It would work. He just needed to get it into the American camp and then get out. It would do damage, but it would also send the message he wanted to send and for that, he was happy. After adding the finishing touches for his bomb, he packed up the things in his house that he would need, and waited for nightfall.

Chapter Fourteen

As darkness slowly overtook the land, TJ, Roberts, and the rest of the Marines all went to their respective posts. They settled into their positions and waited. None of them expected anything to happen tonight, but they knew the stakes, so their guard was up anyway.

Dhul Fiqar had every possession he cared about sitting by his door. He was aware of the need for a quick escape. He exited the building with his bomb on his back and crept towards the American camp.

He finally made it to a hill overlooking the camp, and after waiting for thirty minutes he saw the headlights he was looking for.

The Americans were finally leaving. They were abandoning their camp, and when they came back there would be very little left. He wished he could set a more lethal trap, but the damage done to the camp would be good enough. Plus, he didn't want the Americans to be around and start a man-hunt with him still in the area.

He watched the trucks disappear into the distance, leaned back into the hill, and stared at the sky. It was a clear night and he had a great view of the stars. He stared into the heavens and watched the celestial bodies glisten and shine.

After convincing himself that he had waited long enough, he ended his stargazing with a sigh, then stood up and walked to the camp. As he approached its edge, he checked for any personnel that might have stayed behind. To his relief he found that he was the only one remaining. He located what he assumed was the middle of the camp and began to work. He pulled the makeshift bomb off of his back and placed it onto the ground.

Chapter Fifteen

The crackle of the walkie-talkie made TJ jump.

"Hey, we got a local here. He's just sitting down now, but he's got some stuff with him."

"Keep an eye on him," TJ said.

"Will do." the voice responded.

"Could this be the guy?" TJ wondered silently. "Would he be brazen enough to come so soon?"

Once again TJ's thoughts were interrupted by the buzz of the walkie-talkie.

"Hey, this guy is at the camp. He looks like a local just out exploring, but he's got something with him. I just can't see what it is."

"Okay, keep an eye..." TJ was once again interrupted by the walkie-talkie.

"Scratch that! He is the guy. He's trying to plant a bomb. Everyone in your positions." the voice commanded.

TJ scrambled to his feet. After picking up his pistol, he silently crept up the hill towards the camp. With his new vantage point he was able to spy on the man.

After watching the man for mere moments TJ knew he was the bomber they were tracking. He slid and shifted down the sandy mound to approach the man.

Dhul Fiqar was almost done. He would be clear of this place, and it would be destroyed. The only thing he had left to do was activate the bomb. He was careful not to activate it until the very last moment. If any accident happened, if the switch was hit, the bomb would audibly click, but until the last piece was properly connected that click wouldn't spark an explosion. When he was about to begin that final process, he heard a noise to his side.

He turned and saw a man about fifteen yards away. He was approaching with a weapon drawn, aiming at him. Dhul knew that the main American forces were gone, and that there would be few Americans around. But he also knew there would be many more around soon. No doubt his actions had already been reported and Americans would be heading back. It was obvious, either Dhul or the other man was not going to survive this encounter.

Dhul lifted his hands in surrender, all the while clutching the detonator as the man cautiously approached. He took a couple steps backward.

TJ continued his tentative approach. The man had begun to back away. TJ knew the bomber wouldn't just give up in surrender, but the man's calmness put TJ on edge even more than the situation naturally did.

When the man with the gun stepped past the bomb, Fiqar clicked the detonator. It had worked. The man with the gun jumped and swung around, looking behind him. Fiqar was at full speed before the man was able to turn around.

TJ spun around, but it was too late. The man was tackling him into the ground. After a couple brutal punches to the face TJ started to lose his grip on his gun.

Dhul Fiqar knew he had to disarm the man. With a knee directly on the man's chest he, swiped at the gun and knocked it out of his hands. He then unsheathed his knife. He was going to kill this man silently, detonate the bomb, and leave.

TJ knew his grip on his gun had weakened, and the man would be able to take it from him if he tried. He kept his composure as the gun was knocked from his right hand, while picking up sand in his left hand. The man got on top of him and began to pull out a knife. TJ used his chance to turn the fight back into his favor. He tossed the sand into his attacker's face and used his momentum to throw the attacker off of him.

Stunned, and unable to see, Dhul fell onto his back, landing on the gun.

It couldn't have worked out worse for TJ. The man had landed on TJ's weapon while still retaining control of his knife. This was a fight he couldn't win, but with the man still recovering TJ was able to get to his feet first. As the man stood, TJ was able to swipe at his legs knocking him to the ground once more. The man lunged towards TJ and was able to slice at TJ's leg. The blade caught the side of his leg, cutting him. TJ had to get away- he had to regain the advantage, so he fled, to the caves he had visited a couple days before.

Dhul jumped and gave chase to the other man. After a few steps of running, he realized he was gaining on the American. Dhul had an easier time traversing the terrain. As a result he had already cut the distance between them in half.

The American made it down a hill before disappearing into a small, rocky cave. Dhul had him trapped, and he knew it. The American didn't know these caves like he did, and that would be the reason he would leave the cave alive while the American would lay lifeless in this, this tomb of his choosing.

Dhul slowed to a trot then walked into the cave. He breathed silently so the American wouldn't be able to locate him.

Dhul froze, hoping to hear the American, but he made no noise either. He had to find him. He wouldn't be able to finish with the bomb until he did. Clenching his knife, Dhul turned to his right and silently walked toward the wall of the cave.

There was a scraping sound behind him. Dhul turned, ready to attack the American should he be standing behind him. He wasn't. He stalked to the opposite wall of the cave. He knew the American was hiding there.

He heard another noise come from the wall of the cave he was walking towards. He heard the noise again, a scraping sound, and he quickened his pace.

Suddenly, something metallic fell to the ground behind him, and he turned to confront it. Dhul heard the noise again. He swung his knife in the direction of the sound. But as he did the cave was suddenly fully illuminated, blinding Dhul. An explosion shook the cave and made Dhul fall to the ground. No matter how much he tried to move, his brain and body would not work together.

He couldn't see anything. Dhul was completely blinded. Whimpering in pain, he raised his hands to cover his ears and felt something oozing from them.

As the blood was pouring out of his ears his arms were pulled behind him. He was then sent violently onto the ground.

Dhul Fiqar had been captured by the Americans.

Chapter Sixteen

TJ finally pushed himself off of the ground. He looked to the center of the cave, and he saw a few Marines dragging the bomber out.

The plan had worked, not the way they drew it up, but it had worked nonetheless. After they had cut the lights to the camp, most of the Marines had piled into the transport trucks only to jump out moments later. They were going to enter the surrounding caves and wait for the signal, but by the time they were able to hike back to the camp. TJ had already engaged the man. They had to use plan B. TJ and the other scout had to figure out a way to detonate the flashbang with the man inside the cave. TJ had done so. The Marines hustled to the caves in time to see and hear the explosion. They then poured into the cave and subdued the man.

"Not exactly according to plan but it'll work. Anyone have some bandages?" TJ asked.

"Yeah. We got some, Roberts told TJ.

TJ watched the bomber exit the cave while he bandaged his arm. He then began to relax. It was over. They had the bomber, and he wouldn't be able to cause any more harm.

One group would stay behind and tear the camp down. The second group would leave now and transport the man back to the base.

TJ and Roberts would be in the second group. They both secretly wished the flashbang hadn't incapacitated the bomber as much as it had. They wanted him to try something so they had an excuse to physically stop him.

They threw the man onto the floor in the back of the truck. The first Marine climbed in and, as he stepped over the bomber he kicked him. The rest of the Marines followed suit.

With his hands tied up, Dhul had no way to protect himself. He had to endure a kick from each man that passed- some in the ribs and chest, others in the face, and some on the legs.

They rode back to camp. It was mostly quiet, and some of the men were laughing at how bloodied the bomber had become.

The truck hit a large bump, which sent the man up into the air and violently crashing down onto his face. His nose began to gush blood, covering his face. A Marine reached down to grab him and pull him back onto his side but his hand was gently nudged away by

Roberts' foot. The man nodded, and sat back up, leaving the bomber in his pool of blood.

TJ began to feel bad for the blood-covered man lying by his feet. But, after one thought of what had happened at the station, TJ no longer felt that way.

He felt as if the man was getting off easy.

Dhul heard the men laughing at him. He was angry and embarrassed. He was face first in his own blood. He had become a laughing-stock, a joke. His enemies no longer feared him-they laughed at him. He took comfort in the fantasy that an IED would kill everyone in the truck as it traveled, but it was a wish that didn't come to fruition.

When the truck finally stopped at the base and the bomber was dragged away, TJ and Roberts began to talk.

"Well, it's been a pleasure working with you. Hopefully we'll meet up again sometime," Roberts said.

"With leadership like yours, I would be very surprised if there weren't big things in your future. I just hope you remember my name when you're in charge of all the big decisions."

The men shared a laugh and shook hands before going their separate ways.

TJ sat down on his bed, exhausted. He pulled out a couple of pills and swallowed them with ease.

He felt a wave of relief rush over him. They had captured the bomber and he would no longer be able to harm anyone. TJ threw his shirt to the ground before slipping his pants off and lying on the bed.

He relaxed and fell asleep without a problem.

When he opened his eyes, everything was dark. He looked around and saw a small opening where light was shining in. He took a step to it but when he did a shadow rushed in.

He jumped back and found that he was standing against the wall of a cave. He put his arm up and found the wire. TJ grabbed it and let it lead him to the crevice.

He paused and looked at what the bomber was doing. His back was to TJ. He could pull his gun out and force the bomber to surrender.

He reached for his gun, but it was wedged between him and the wall. He would have to come back out of the crevice to free his weapon. It was harder to move out, and it felt like the walls were closing in on him.

TJ had to focus back on the bomber instead of his overwhelming claustrophobia. He glanced back at the man and was horrified to see what he had been doing. The man stood to his feet and turned and stared at TJ. There was a bomb at his feet and a detonator in his hand. The man smiled and began to laugh maniacally.

TJ stepped out of the crevice to run away but tripped to the ground. As he looked back at the bomber time seemed to slow down.

The man continued laughing as his finger pressed the trigger. The man's laughter grew louder as the flames jumped around him. The flesh on his face began to melt away.

TJ felt the heat approaching him and cringed as the heat overtook his body.

The man had somehow remained standing and, his laughter continued even as his hair was gone and his face was melting when his eye exploded in flames. It too began to melt until the only thing left of the man's head was his skull with a small flame kindling in the eye sockets.

As the fire neared TJ, he felt the flames sear his body. He tried to raise his arm to protect himself, but he couldn't. The man's body approached with continued laughter. Flames once more jumped from behind the man and onto TJ.

TJ woke up and tried to escape the burning sensation that he felt. He was covered in sweat. It was the middle of the day, and his room had trapped in the heat. He stood and went to shower.

After doing so, he strolled through the camp trying to get rid of the ghastly images that still were in his head when a voice called to him from behind. It was Phillip.

"Hey TJ. Come here. I need to talk to you."

"What's up?" TJ asked.

"First off, nice job catching the bomber. He is going to be transported to a beautiful island where he will receive the best treatment available. Second, you're going to be heading out of here pretty soon. We got a call and you're going to be working with CIA now. I don't know when they'll get ahold of you, but you'll get to go home for a bit before then."

TJ thanked Phillip before jogging back to his room. He pulled out his laptop and quickly emailed Emy to tell her he would be home soon.

Even though he had slept most of the day his dreams had prevented him from getting much rest. He lay back on his bed knowing that soon he would be reunited with his wife.

Chapter Seventeen

As TJ took his seat on the plane, he couldn't help but to feel guilty. He had been here for only a few days and was, already able to go home. He knew there were others more worthy of going home than he was. He knew everyone there had been deployed for much longer. Yet he was going home, and they weren't. Some of them might not even make it home. TJ shuddered at the thought.

As the plane left the ground, TJ felt relieved. He was leaving: he was actually leaving. He had been away for much longer times before, but, unlike those times, he now had a burning desire for home and to be with the woman that awaited him.

He thought back to when he and Emy had finally moved in together. They had decided that to save money, she would move her stuff into his apartment and they would save until they were able to find a house.

It was the week after their honeymoon. He drove the U-Haul truck to her apartment with her right beside him, holding his hand the whole way. When they walked through the doors, they found that everything was already packed up and in boxes. She told TJ that her parents had stayed in her apartment and had packed her things for her.

They both began to take boxes out and load them into the U-Haul,

Emy placed a box into the truck and hurried back into the apartment as TJ picked up another box.

"Do you need me to pick that up for you? Is it too heavy?" Emy teased.

"If you think you can handle it." TJ handed her the box, while laughing, then proceeded to pick up a much lighter one.

"Wow, that's very manly of you, taking that box and leaving me with this one," Emy joked as she led him out the door.

"Well, I am a specimen of manliness." TJ said, while following her down the stairs. "Just watch, I'm so manly that I can catch it too."

TJ then flipped the box into the air and as he stepped forward to catch it, he slipped and fell down the few remaining stairs. Emy was watching and was able to get out of his way as he came crashing down.

After seeing that he was okay she continued to joke saying, "You're right, that was extremely manly." Emy laughed as she walked away.

"I told you you'd be impressed!" TJ yelled after her. He lay on the ground for a couple seconds before getting back up and loading the rest of the boxes.

Emy, however, continued to ask him to prove his manliness by carrying other boxes. TJ got it. He wasn't annoyed by her bringing up his fall. He knew that he had deserved the teasing.

After packing everything into the truck, they drove back to his apartment, their apartment. They left the same way they had arrived, hand in hand the whole time.

TJ and Emy each unloaded a couple boxes and walked up to his door. Emy arrived first and put her boxes on the ground so she could open the door. Once she unlocked it, TJ dropped his boxes so he could pick her up in his arms and carried her across the threshold.

Sudden turbulence shook TJ away from his thoughts and back to the reality inside the plane. They were beginning their descent.

The plane landed at Ramstein Air Force Base. TJ waited there for a couple hours before finally boarding another military plane to go back stateside.

When it came time to board the next plane TJ ended up in the back of the line. He found a pair of empty window seats near the back of the plane.

TJ stared out of his window and watched the ground slowly distance itself, before being replaced by clouds.

TJ awoke to the flight attendant's voice coercing him out of sleep. He opened his eyes and saw her. She was standing beside him, her hand on his shoulder gently shaking him awake.

"Sir, are you okay?" The attendant asked.

Even though his heart was still pounding and his body was drenched in sweat, TJ assured her he was all right. He had had another nightmare, but thankfully, this time he didn't remember much. There were only a few details he did recall. An amazingly bright landscape, almost cartoonish in color. Shadows, he never saw her but he knew it was the shadow of Emy moving away from him. Yelling. He didn't know where it came from or what was going on, but it had left him shaken.

It took some time before the attendant reluctantly accepted TJ's excuses. He was fine. That's what he told her, and what he would have to continue telling himself. While TJ may have convinced the flight attendant, he hadn't convinced himself. He was losing his sanity, but he had to act as if he was completely normal in order to maintain any continuity in his life. If he lost his job because of this, he had nowhere to turn. Yeah, Emy was there, but the relationship could only handle so much strain before breaking.

TJ didn't want to think about it. The thought of losing Emy and literally everything he knew was horrible. Emy and his job were the only things he cared about.

As TJ exited the plane he saw a man staring at him, almost as if he were studying him. TJ walked towards him.

He greeted Tucker who then welcomed TJ back to the United States before sitting down to talk briefly.

They spoke quietly of TJ's PTSD and his struggles with it. Tucker asked if he had taken his special medication and TJ told him he hadn't since he started his return home. Tucker frowned and implored TJ to take it regularly and keep track of the results. TJ assured him that he would. With that, Tucker left to get in line for a plane departing to Seattle.

"That was odd." TJ thought. *"How did he know I would be coming through here? Did someone send him?"*

TJ stared out of the airport windows and observed the rainy Philadelphia day while pondering these possibilities.

He would soon board his final plane. His plane to Des Moines. His plane home.

Chapter Eighteen

TJ landed in Des Moines and almost ran over the other passengers in his rush to get off of the plane. He made his way through the airport and finally found Emy.

She was wearing a pair of jeans and a green sweater. He rushed towards her and they threw their arms around each other. Emy held her head to TJ's chest, she was ecstatic to see him. TJ ran his hand through her hair and kissed her on the forehead.

She was happy to see him and to welcome him back to the comforts of home. But after she noticed how weary he was, she began to wonder what had happened. Emy knew that TJ struggled with PTSD and often had bouts of nightmares.

TJ had promised when they got married that he would be honest with her about his PTSD. He had been mostly open with her, but she could still tell when he was struggling. He would tell her but he would usually spare the details.

Emy took his hand and led him to their car. TJ sat in the passenger seat and was able to relax. He had comfortable surroundings, his car, his town, and most importantly, his wife.

TJ turned the radio on and decided he would have some fun with Emy. He would let one song play on each station before changing it to the next. He was going to see how long it took for her to notice. It comforted him to feel and act the way he had before the PTSD.

Emy knew what he was doing, but she wasn't annoyed by it. It was nice to know that her husband was still able to have a bit of fun. Another song ended, and as TJ reached to change the station, Emy's hand caught his and brought it to her leg. She held his hand the whole drive back home.

When they arrived at the apartment, they entered and TJ plopped onto the couch with Emy. A short while later there was a knock at the door. TJ glanced at Emy before getting up.

He opened the door to find a Pizza Hut delivery man holding a box and a two liter Pepsi. TJ turned back to Emy, who smiled and said, "I hope it's okay, I didn't want to make anything, and plus it's your favorite."

TJ paid the man and took the food. Emy and TJ ate together, watched TV, and talked about the events of the past few days.

TJ was tired, so they went to bed early that night. Emy slept peacefully, but TJ, as usual, tossed and turned before violently waking up because of a bad dream. He accidentally woke Emy up when he jumped, gasping.

TJ was then forced to confess that he was still having trouble with dreams, not just dreams, but telling reality from his delusions. He told her that he felt guilty, guilty for the lives that had been lost. He told her about the fight with the Marine on the base. He also admitted to feeling inadequate.

"Face it," he continued, "I'm losing it, and it's getting worse every day. You shouldn't be with me. I'm just making things harder for you."

As TJ struggled to get the words out of his mouth, she interrupted him, telling him that she would stick by his side no matter what.

She knew TJ wasn't normally like this. He was speaking nonsense, most likely a mix of the PTSD and of how tired he was. Most of what he was saying was probably exaggerated. She knew her husband couldn't sleep well outside of home, and because of that she assumed that he hadn't been able to rest on the way home at all and was still attempting to unwind. It might take a couple days, but soon Emy knew he would be back to his normal self.

It was now four in the morning. They sat in their darkened room talking before he followed her to the living room couch. They sat down and continued to talk, but soon they were both overcome by fatigue.

Instead of going back to the bed, TJ lay on the couch and draped his arm over Emy who snuggled closer to him. As TJ fell back asleep, he was still aware of the warmth of her body pressing against him. When he entered his dreams, that presence kept him grounded in reality.

When they awoke, he told her what had happened and how sleeping on the couch with her had helped him combat his nightmares. Their conversation soon shifted to TJ's job.

"I'm gonna have to go back, TJ whispered.

"Already? You just got back."

"I just left, too. I know it isn't ideal, but I was at least able to come back. That's more than most others get."

"How long will you be gone this time?"

"Until they don't need me anymore. I don't really know when that will be."

They continued talking before eating some leftover pizza for breakfast.

It had been a good few days for TJ. He was able to go the whole time without taking his PTSD pills, and he actually felt better. They slept on the couch each night, and TJ figured that was the reason for the sudden improvement.

They arrived at the airport, and TJ walked to the back of the car and took out his suitcase and a duffel bag.

Emy knew the job fit TJ well and was something he had felt called to do. But, she loathed the effects it had had on his mind. She was also afraid of the way it might hurt their marriage if they didn't handle it right.

Chapter Nineteen

TJ looked through the glass doors and watched Emy drive away. He made it through security and found his gate. He looked down at his travel itinerary. He would leave Des Moines in one hour, then fly to Nashville. From there he would go to Tampa Bay and then on to London. From London he would fly to Istanbul then to Tel Aviv.

He knew that this curious flight plan was given to him for a reason. It was to ensure TJ would notice if he was being followed. None of these flights were as direct as they should have been, which meant, that another passenger could not board every plane TJ did without his noticing.

By the time TJ made it to Tampa Bay, all of the passengers who had been with him on earlier flights were no longer traveling with him. With the knowledge that he wasn't being followed, TJ relaxed and decided to grab a bite to eat.

After eating, TJ boarded his plane to London.

He wondered when the next time he would see American soil again would be. He knew there was always a possibility that he wouldn't see American soil again. He had, in fact, grown accustomed to the thought of never coming back. The thought of death no longer bothered TJ. He felt that whenever he was going to die he would calmly embrace it. TJ watched out the window as Raymond James Stadium disappeared, then leaned back in his seat and fell asleep.

He opened his eyes and looked at Emy as she walked towards him. He was sitting on a park bench waiting for her.

She smiled just like always, then froze in her tracks and looked at him. Her mouth slowly dropped, and her face contorted in pain. Shocked, TJ stood up to go to help her, but as he did he saw white spikes protruding from her abdomen.

Everything then happened in slow motion.

Her body was lifted off of the ground. Behind her stood the creature. It seemed to be laughing as its antlers held her body high. Gravity, slowly and painfully, brought her body down farther on the antlers. She opened her mouth to cry out in pain, but TJ only heard her gargle and choke on her blood.

The creature flung its head forward throwing, her pierced and bloody body to the ground. It then looked up at TJ. He stared into the blackness of its eye sockets as the creature began to charge.

TJ reached down for his pistol but slipped on the grip, an error which cost him precious time. He grabbed for his gun again, pulled it from its holster, and clicked the safety off in one smooth motion. He then raised it and pulled the trigger. A small explosion forced the bullet out of the barrel. He saw it make contact and bounce off of the skull.

He fired again. Another explosion. He pulled the trigger yet again. All three shots hit the skull on target, but none slowed the creature. TJ steadied his aim for a fourth and final shot. He leveled his gun with the creature's eye sockets.

Just then the creature's antlers pierced TJ's abdomen. He felt them as they pushed through his body and broke the skin on his back. He felt the antlers invade his body as the creature raised him above itself, and he began the painful slide down. He watched as another antler of the deer came closer and closer to his face. He tried to pull his head back to get away but, he didn't have the strength. His head fell forward, and the last thing TJ felt was the antler penetrating his eye.

TJ jolted upright in his seat before hurrying to the bathroom. He felt sick. He wanted to throw up and forget the dream, but he knew that neither was likely to happen. He stood over the toilet, waiting. He was sweaty, and his stomach was tight. He put his hands against the wall to brace himself as he leaned forward ready to vomit, but nothing happened. He stood motionless for a few more seconds, hoping to either throw up or regain his composure enough to return to his seat.

He eventually sat on the toilet and put his head in his hands. He exhaled heavily. TJ tried to control his breathing to help calm himself, but his mind was still watching Emy, then himself, get impaled by the creature.

A few minutes later he heard a knock on the door and someone asked if the bathroom was occupied. TJ was forced to stand up and make his way back to his seat.

TJ nervously waited for the plane to land. He wanted to sleep, but every time he closed his eyes he saw Emy being attacked by the creature. He stared out of his window into the blackness of night. Below him was a dark ocean. Even the inside of the plane was darkened to make sleep easier. TJ watched the night sky, looking at the clouds as they passed through them. He didn't know how long he had been asleep he just wanted to land.

Two mundane hours passed before it did. There was very little traffic inside or around the London airport. One or two planes took off and landed in the obscurity of night, but the airport felt deserted.

He wondered if he would be working hand in hand with an Israeli counterpart or if he would commit espionage against America's Israeli allies.

He didn't like the fact that he still didn't know what was happening. He didn't know what to prepare for, especially since he wasn't going back to Afghanistan or Iraq like he normally did.

He pulled a couple of pills from his pocket and took them. Now the only thing he could do was wait for the next flight. Thankfully, the time passed quickly, and he was soon able to board the plane.

The flight was nice and uneventful, just the way TJ liked it. Before long he was landing in Istanbul.

He was weary from his travels. He longed to be in Tel Aviv so that he could try to get some rest. He looked and felt like a zombie, slowly dragging along as he walked.

Four hours later he was approaching Tel Aviv. The city was bathed in sunlight, and the Mediterranean Sea sparkled like a pool of diamonds below him. It was a truly beautiful sight and he made a mental note that, when he was traveling for leisure, Tel Aviv would be at the top of his list.

Chapter Twenty

It was the first time that TJ would work directly with the CIA. He normally worked for the DOD and once he had been with the FBI and DOJ for a mission. TJ held no official job title in the United States government. He had no single organization that he belonged to. He was a government agent, that would work for, and with whomever needed him. He was just an asset to them, moving him whenever and to wherever they needed him. Right now they needed him in Tel Aviv.

TJ picked up his bags as he was approached by a man. The man introduced himself and told TJ he would be driving him to the Dan Panorama Tel Aviv, the hotel where TJ would be staying.

TJ cautiously followed the man to a cab and climbed into the back seat.

After about a half hour of driving, the taxi pulled into the Dan Panorama. TJ thanked and paid the driver before getting out. He was immediately met by one of the hotel workers who, insisted on taking TJ's bags for him.

TJ gave the man his bags and asked for a key to his room, explaining that he wanted to go sightseeing first.

The worker nodded, handed TJ a key to room 1527, and hustled away with TJ's things. TJ knew the CIA wouldn't risk directly contacting him so quickly after arriving.

He decided to turn and walk down near the shore of the Mediterranean. He strolled along the beach until he found a small restaurant.

He sat on the terrace and ate the most American thing he could find on the menu all while enjoying his view of the sea. The sea air that filled TJ's lungs was invigorating. Even though he had not been able to sleep much in his travels he was now fully awake.

He walked back to the hotel after he ate. The spray of the sea came across TJ as he ambled down the beach. He finally made it back to the hotel and was met by the same concierge who had taken his bags earlier.

He entered the hotel and took an elevator up to the fifteenth floor. He found and entered his room and was amazed at the sight that greeted him. The window was open, and the sun illuminated the waters below. The glistening sea was beautiful.

He picked up his bags and placed them on the bed before inspecting the whole room looking for surveillance bugs. When he was convinced there were none, he lay on his bed and relaxed.

When TJ got up, he opened his bags and found an envelope that he hadn't put there. Before opening it, he carefully examined it for any signs of hidden danger. Convinced it was safe, he pulled out and read the instructions.

He would spend a day acting as a tourist, blending in, before he would be contacted and moved.

TJ was happy with the news. He would get to spend a day at this beautiful location and actually be able to enjoy the area for a bit.

He left the hotel again and found a small shop on the beach. There he purchased a towel, sunscreen, and swimming trunks. He then left the shop in search of a secluded part of the beach.

After finding a spot, he dug a small hole in the sand, put his possessions into it, and covered them with his towel. He then walked down to the water and began to swim. He didn't recognize it, but the water had pulled him away from the shore. After making the exhausting swim back to the beach. He picked up his towel and the rest of his things and walked back to the hotel.

Chapter Twenty-One

He once again entered his room and walked into the bathroom. He had noticed the Jacuzzi tub earlier and knew he would want to take advantage of it. He turned on the water and began to take off his clothes. He walked back into his room and tossed his clothes onto the bed. TJ returned to a mostly full bath and checked the water temperature. It was nice and cool, just the way he liked it.

He stepped into the tub and slowly lowered himself. The cool water shocked his body, but he quickly adjusted.

He turned the jets on and situated himself in the tub. TJ leaned back and slipped down until the water came over his mouth and up to his nose. It was relaxing. Especially after the exhausting swim.

His relaxation was cut short, however, when there was a crash inside of his bedroom.

TJ stood as a man threw the door open and rushed him. As TJ tried to step out of the tub, the man tackled him back against the wall. Both men landed with a hard thud, and a splash.

TJ was underwater, facing his attacker. He could feel the man's hands holding him under. He swung a violent haymaker that grazed the man's jaw. As the man's grip on TJ weakened, TJ threw a left-handed punch at the man's elbow. The impact and the loss of stability caused the man to collapse into the tub landing on TJ.

TJ pushed the man to the side and then jerked his own head up out of the tub to gasp for air. He inhaled a mix of air and water. As he coughed the water out, the man pushed him back under.

He needed to resurface quickly to stay conscious. He hadn't brought in enough air and, his lungs were burning. The man was pushing him down in the tub, so TJ quickly rolled to his side, forcing the man to tumble in after him.

TJ lunged to the surface again but the man's arm caught his jugular forcing a reactionary gasp for air. Water filled his mouth and flowed to his burning lungs. He tried to spit the water out but only inhaled more.

TJ had one final chance. He lurched for the surface and opened his mouth. His gasp for air was the only audible thing in the bathroom. He sat up in the tub shaking and looked around. There was no sign of his attacker.

He sat in the tub a moment longer, trying to regain his composure before he trusted his legs enough to step out.

He grabbed a towel before wobbling into the bedroom. The door was closed, and nothing was out of place. He uneasily lay down onto his bed and began to weep. TJ didn't understand how a man like him, who had gone through as much training as he had, could be so scared. He felt weak and helpless and, worst of all, alone.

He contemplated telling a superior how bad his PTSD had gotten, but he knew that doing so would result in him losing his job. That's something he didn't want to put his new family through. As he cried, he rolled over on his bed and looked at his bag.

TJ had forgotten to take his pills again, so he reached out to locate them. He pulled the bag closer to feel around inside for the pills. When he found them, he opened the bottle and dumped the contents into his hand. Pills fell from his hand and bounced to the bed and floor while three others remained in his grasp.

TJ hesitantly brought the few pills up to his mouth and swallowed. He struggled to get them down, which caused a fit of coughing before the pills all came tumbling back out of his mouth.

He picked up a pill from off of his bed and swallowed it. He lay back against his pillow with tears still streaming down his face. He wished it all would end, no matter what the cost.

He began to ponder what could offer his mind true freedom from the nightmares. He started to pick up pills off of his bed, the three he had tried to swallow earlier and the others that had fallen when he had dumped them all out. He filled his hand-nine pills in total and-hesitantly asked himself if these pills could liberate his mind.

He knew they could. It wasn't a question that needed to be asked. All he had to do was swallow them and wait for them to take effect.

He pulled out his phone and wiped tears out of his eyes so he could see. He looked at pictures of himself and Emy together. He wanted his last thoughts to be good ones.

He paused and admired a picture of her in her wedding dress. Her smile was beautiful.

TJ then thought of how hard it would be on Emy if he took these pills. She might even blame herself for his death. He couldn't put her through that heartache, even if there was nothing she could do to help him. She was the only reason he still had for living, but she was reason enough.

He threw the pills across the room and into the wall. He then lay back down and continued to cry. TJ kept looking at pictures of Emy, hoping that they would provide encouragement for him, but the only thing they brought was crushing guilt. Guilt that he would put his needs and wants so much higher than hers and guilt that he could be selfish enough to consider committing suicide and abandoning her.

He put his phone down and closed his eyes. There was no way to get comfortable; his brain wouldn't let him. The emotional and psychological roller coaster he was riding fatigued his mind and body.

TJ's head rested on his damp pillow as he dozed off. He awoke covered in sweat before falling back to sleep. This cycle and his nightmares continued until the next morning.

Not being able to recall the nightmares had helped him ease back into sleep but had made it all the more disheartening when he awoke again.

He was roused by the sound of a ringing telephone. He rolled over and answered it.

"Hello." he said.

"TJ, you up?"

"Yeah, yeah, I'm up now."

"My name is Anthony Yallsten. Come down to the hotel restaurant in thirty minutes. Get a table for three and we'll meet you there."

"Okay, sounds good. I'll be there."

The mysterious voice on the other side of the phone hung up.

TJ didn't have to wait long to be seated. The waiter led him to a small round table surrounded by four chairs. He chose the one that would give him the best view of the entrance.

As he waited, he silently reflected on what had happened the night before. He didn't know what to do. The pills didn't seem to be helping, but he knew he wasn't taking them consistently.

He was fearful that as his dreams became more realistic they would increasingly blur the line of reality. It terrified him that his condition had progressed that far without warning. He hoped that it wouldn't happen again, even though he knew in the pit of his stomach that it would.

TJ then felt a hand on his shoulder, causing him to jump. He turned to see a small Israeli man and taller American standing behind him. The American was of average height and had short dark hair. He didn't have any noticeable features about him, and TJ figured that, as a CIA operative, that was a nice trait. The Israeli, however, was a short man, but what he lacked in height he made up for in muscle.

"TJ, nice to meet you." The American said.

"I hope he is more observant than he has proven to be so far." the Israeli man whispered.

The two men sat down by TJ and began to talk.

"Obviously, we can't explain everything to you here. So let's eat and then we will take you to Kinneret." the Israeli said.

The American extended his hand to TJ. "Anthony Yallsten, we spoke earlier."

"You already know who I am, but it's nice to meet you," TJ said while shaking the man's hand.

The waiter came to the table and took the men's orders. They sat in silence for the most of their meal, knowing that the conversation worth having would come later.

After breakfast, TJ rushed to his room and grabbed his things before meeting the men in the parking lot. He put his bags in the back of the car then climbed into the back seat.

"Okay, as you already know I am CIA," Yallsten explained. "This is David Tabor and he's an Israeli commando. We've found signs of a suspected terrorist training facility in Georgia, the country"

"There is nothing suspected about it!" Tabor interrupted, "It is there!"

"I know it is, sorry." Yallsten apologized. "It isn't a question of whether or not it's there.

What we are doing and have been doing is trying to figure out more about it. You got here just in time for the easy part."

"That he did," Tabor agreed.

"Why are we here then?"

"Gathering intel, our next source of intel is going to be a couple members of a terrorist cell this camp has produced. They decided they liked money more than ideology. After we get what we need from them we'll be able to formulate a plan from there."

"There have been four of us from the CIA, but one of our guys was removed from the mission, that's why you were brought in." Yallsten continued. "You will join us as we finish up our work. This is a joint operation between us, the Israeli Commandos, and our Navy SEALs. The Israelis are getting as much intel as they can via satellite and other overhead images. The SEALs are training with the Commandos, waiting for the call to go in. We're getting the intel from these guys in order to relay that to the SEALs and Commandos. We'll let them decide what to do with it."

The call to bring the SEALs in came in from the head of the DOD. It didn't really bother the Israelis or the CIA. Each knew that the SEALs would bring a deadly tenacity to any situation they were in. The Commandos regularly interacted with SEALs, so it felt natural for the two groups to work together again.

"None of us will be on the ground for an attack?" TJ asked.

"That's the hope," Yallsten responded.

"Using the intel you bring us on the camp will prepare us to wipe out any resistance we could encounter," Tabor said.

Yallsten nodded, then continued. "We hope to have a small centralized command team when the attack commences. It will consist of two Commandos, two SEALs, and two of us. We'll all work together to sort through the intel, that's the group we want you in. But then again, the plan all depends on the intel we bring in. Heck, it could be a group of farmers living together peacefully."

Yallsten began to chuckle, but the glare he received form Tabor convinced him not to.

"I've had it happen before," Yallsten tried to defend his joke, but Tabor was having none of it.

"The *camp*," Tabor stressed," is in the mountains surrounded by trees. That's why this intel you are going to get is so important. We have twenty Commandos, fourteen SEALs, and now, with you, four CIA operatives."

"Overkill?" TJ asked.

"With men like this, there is no such thing. We not only have strength in numbers but flexibility as well. We can attack from any or all directions at once if we need to," Tabor said.

TJ realized that he had a valid point.

The car came to a stop, and Tabor and TJ exited the vehicle.

"This is where I leave you all," Tabor said.

TJ climbed into the front seat and watched as Tabor walked away and out of sight behind a group of buildings.

"Interesting character," TJ said.

"He isn't too bad once he warms up to you."

The two men shared a laugh before Yallsten continued to explain the mission to TJ.

"So, from our preliminary surveillance, we suspect anywhere from twenty to fifty men at the camp at all times. The Israelis have spotted more in and out traffic recently, so it will probably be closer to fifty."

"We aren't sure of their numbers? Even with satellite?" TJ asked.

"No, the camp is surrounded by woods and has a lot of tree cover. We're picking up in and out traffic but can't get an accurate estimate of their forces." Yallsten continued, "These guys aren't going to be a bunch of scrubs. These are guys that after they get trained they're sent to hit Israel. So we're going to stop it before they have the chance to do any real damage. We don't expect them to be ready for us to take the offensive, so if we hit them first, while they don't expect it, we'll end up with a camp full of dead terrorists, and that my friend, is a nice thing."

"Yeah, it is," TJ concluded.

Chapter Twenty-Two

When they arrived in Kinneret, TJ soon found himself in an apartment room with Anthony and two other men he had yet to meet.

One of the men sat on the couch reviewing papers, and the other paced near the window. The man on the couch didn't bother to look up when Yallsten and TJ entered the room, but the tall black man at the window approached them.

"So," he said. "This is TJ."

"Yeah," TJ extended his arm and shook the man's hand.

"My name is Vincent Davy. It's good to meet you."

"Good to meet you as well."

Davy was tall and lanky. He carried himself with a certain confidence that not many others had. He had a soft voice that still somehow conveyed strength.

The man on the couch stood up. He had graying hair and just enough facial hair to be noticeable. One look at him and TJ could tell he was a leader who took his leadership seriously.

He introduced himself as Evert Oden. The two men shook hands, then Oden returned to his seat to continue studying the papers.

As TJ inquired about the plan, he was informed that he and Vincent would most likely be the two inside the joint operation command.

Oden turned to Yallsten. "Are you ready to go now?"

"Yeah, I got my things ready before we picked TJ up."

"Head out in thirty?"

"Works for me. You finalize everything while I was gone?"

The look Yallsten received from Oden was all he needed in order to know that was a stupid question to ask.

"What's going on?" TJ asked the men.

"Me and Alst are going to meet with one of our informants. You and Davy will pick us up in six hours. We will relay whatever intel we get to the Israelis and SEALs and move from there. Hopefully we will be able to get this over with in the next couple of days. You showed up for the easy part of this."

"That's what I've been told," TJ admitted.

"Davy knows where to pick us up, so I think that that pretty much covers it."

Oden walked to the bathroom, and TJ took his seat on the couch. He began to look over the papers, focusing on the area of the maps where the camp was located. He continued his study until Oden and Yallsten were ready to leave.

The three CIA operatives walked to the door before Davy turned back to TJ. "I'm gonna take the guys and drop them off. I should be back in about an hour. I'm sure you're tired from all the traveling, so go ahead and get some sleep. No need to slave over those papers all night. I can fill you in tomorrow."

TJ nodded. "Okay, sounds good."

The three men shuffled out of the door and silently closed it behind them.

TJ stood up and walked to the window to watch the silhouettes of the three men as they approached and entered a car. As he watched the car drive away, TJ decided that he would take Davy's suggestion and try to sleep some. But first, he wanted to look over the papers.

TJ plopped down onto the couch and picked up and studied a map. One thing stood out to him. It was not friendly terrain at all. It was very mountainous, and the tree cover kept the satellite from taking any good pictures.

He continued to look at satellite images and found a few thermal pictures of large trucks driving to and from the camp. These images of the glowing white trucks made TJ grateful for the thermal cameras. He knew that in a normal picture these vehicles would be near impossible to see.

TJ leaned onto his side and relaxed. He rested his head against the arm of the couch and closed his eyes. He was sprawled out and for a brief moment felt tranquil.

He was alerted to the faint sound of movement in the hall followed by the jingling of a lock pick in the door handle. He crept across the room, remaining careful not to make a sound. He stood with his back to the wall adjacent to the door and watched as the door squeaked open. Three men wearing masks entered the room. The last one turned to close the door and TJ immediately punched him in the throat, and he fell down, momentarily paralyzed.

The two other men turned around, but TJ was too fast. He tackled the first man, sending them both falling into the second. The three of them fell to the floor and wrestled around throwing, punches. TJ got hit multiple times but was the first of the three to get back to his feet.

He kicked both of the men but was violently tackled to the floor by the first man he had punched. The man was on top of TJ punching him in the face while TJ struggled to defend himself. TJ was, however, finally able to land a hit on the man. He rolled out from under him and stood to his feet once more.

TJ was then grabbed from behind and slammed down onto the table. The other two men had fully recovered. Once again it was an unfair three versus one fight. TJ was shaken but, he refused to stop fighting.

He rolled backwards off the table towards one of the men while avoiding punches from the other two. He tried to stand but, the man was already throwing TJ back towards the table. Then, as the man forced TJ to backpedal, the table took out his legs and he fell backwards landing on the couch.

TJ was beat. He knew it and so did his attackers. His arms gave out on him as he tried to push himself up off of the couch to continue fighting.

He watched the men as they all began to take off their masks. He was shocked to see Davy's, Oden's, and Yallsten's faces. The very men who he thought he was to be working with just attacked him. Slowly Davy approached TJ with a look of curiosity on his face.

He inched closer to TJ before pushing his shoulder and giving him a light slap on the face.

TJ responded with a brutal uppercut that knocked Davy back onto the table. TJ leaned over ready to punch him again but froze as Davy yelled, "Wait man! It's just me! Calm down!"

TJ looked around. Yallsten and Oden were gone. He looked back down at Davy who had a look of bewilderment on his face. "It's nice to see you've got a real mean killer spirit. There's no screwing with you, man." Davy cautiously laughed before holding his hand out.

TJ grabbed it and helped him off the table.

"Sorry about that, I just really like my beauty sleep."

TJ was thankful to see that Davy didn't take it personally.

"Man, I am never, and I mean never slapping this dude," Davy said laughing.

A short time later, the two began to talk.

"So how did you end up in the CIA?" TJ asked.

"Well, I worked my way up through the Navy after college. I was able to work on quite a few classified information analysis projects. My success with those is what got the CIA's attention and that's why I'm here now."

"Nice. Well here's another one, why did you join the Navy?"

"That's a long story."

"We have time," TJ assured him.

"Okay." Davy sighed. "My father wasn't around when I was young. He had a couple kids then, decided he didn't want anything to do with us. With him out of the picture, mom had to do everything she could to provide for us. She was the one that insisted to name me Vincent. A white man name so I'd get looked at on job applications and stuff like that. She was always thinking ahead like that. But she became too busy trying to provide for us to raise us. With her working two jobs and unable to pay for a babysitter, it was rough.

"I had gotten to the age where school started to become harder for me, and that's when mom took a big risk. She quit her second job, even though she knew it would hurt her future just so she could help me and the rest of us with our school work. I was at the age where I could have started to make some money delivering stuff or just doing other small tasks for the gangbangers. I think mom knew that too, so she quit and really made us all focus on our schooling.

"That's what really got my life started on the right track. I studied hard and eventually found myself at the top of my class. I even had a couple of scholarship offers for football heading into my senior year but I had to quit playing sports so I could get a job. Mom was against it because she wanted me to go to college and knew how much an athletic scholarship would provide.

117

"I finally convinced her that we would be fine without me playing. I was able to keep my grades up without the pressure of sports. So after graduation I had some options, but thanks to an academic full ride I was able to work a job and put that money back into helping my family."

A phone call interrupted him. TJ listened as Davy answered the phone.

"Hello," a pause, "Yeah, we'll be there as soon as we can."

Davy turned to TJ. "Yallsten and Oden aren't liking this meeting."

"Didn't they already meet with the informant?" TJ asked.

"No, I dropped them off a few hours before the meeting so they could get a feel for the area and make sure everything was okay. They've got another hour before the meeting is supposed to take place, but we're going in now."

Chapter Twenty-Three

They had hoped they wouldn't have to use guns tonight, but they were prepared if they had to.

Davy climbed into the driver seat of the car and TJ sat in the passenger seat. Davy then instructed TJ to slide open a hidden compartment that was under his seat.

TJ looked down and smiled at what he saw: two MP5 sub-machine guns, light-weight weapons perfect for close combat.

"If Oden and Yallsten aren't there, we're going to give them ten minutes before we get out and go look for them."

TJ nodded as he picked up and examined his weapon. The MP5s had silencers on them. TJ figured that they had been used before and assumed Yallsten and Oden carried two matching weapons.

Forty minutes later, Davy turned their car lights off. The men slowed down, moving in the shadows as they approached their rendezvous point.

Davy parked the car and leaned forward against the steering wheel. He peered into the night sky, examining the darkness for any sign of Oden and Yallsten. There was sudden movement from the brush.

TJ and Davy watched as Oden and Yallsten slowly approached. Their silhouettes were barely visible. It looked like they were joined at the hip.

Davy and TJ heard yelling.

"Hey, c'mon help us. We've got to get out of here!" TJ and Davy opened their doors and jumped out of the car with their MP5s in hand.

"Yallsten's hit; we need to get going now!"

TJ and Davy rushed over to the men. Yallsten limped alongside Oden with his arm draped over him. Davy and TJ both put their arms around Yallsten and lifted him off the ground.

They carried him back to the car and laid him down in the back seat. He was bleeding- a single bullet had hit him in the leg. There was no exit wound, so they would have to bandage only the entrance point. Davy tossed his gun onto the dashboard and climbed into the back to start providing treatment for Yallsten.

Oden was already in the driver's seat shifting the car into drive when TJ sat down in the passenger seat. He slammed the door as the car shot away.

"What happened?" Davy demanded.

"It was a set up. We were able to avoid the ambush, but we still ended up in a gun fight with a few others. I think we lost them."

"You think?"

"Yes. We aren't sure."

Yallsten cried out in pain as Davy worked on his leg.

TJ looked back at Yallsten just in time to see a black van skid around the corner behind them. The passenger window rolled down, and a man with a gun leaned out.

"Everyone get down!" TJ yelled while ducking.

Davy dove onto Yallsten's body, causing another scream of pain as a burst of gunfire erupted from behind them.

Bullets pelted the back of their car, knocking out a taillight and shattering the back windshield.

When the gunfire ceased, TJ popped up with his weapon in hand, ready to fire. But he knew better than to try to shoot over Yallsten and Davy. He turned to the side and rolled down the window.

"Turn right!" TJ commanded.

"No, we need to go left!" Oden protested.

"I need a shot. I can't get that going left! Turn right!"

Another burst of gunfire from behind caused the men to duck again.

"Turn right!" TJ once again commanded, overriding Oden. As he held his gun up, ready to lean out the window.

Oden turned right, and as their car skidded across the pavement, TJ was able to let off a few bursts of inaccurate shots.

The van came around the corner behind them and continued firing.

"I need these guys off us so I can help Yallsten!" Davy pleaded.

"I need you to turn left!" TJ yelled over the sound of gunfire from behind.

"What?" Oden screamed back.

"Just trust me!" TJ said as he picked up Davy's MP5 and strapped it around his shoulder.

As the gunshots momentarily ceased, TJ hoisted himself up. He braced his chest against the top of the vehicle and pulled both MP5s up onto the top of his vehicle. He picked up one of the guns and aimed down the sight before letting a small burst of fire out at the pursuing van. He hit a headlight, but the other bullets that hit the van did very little damage.

The man in the van behind him leaned out and shot again. TJ couldn't duck back into the car so he put his arm in front of his head and leaned down against the roof of the car.

The turn was coming soon. TJ picked up the other MP5. He knew that his shooting would be sporadic and inaccurate, but he wanted to keep the pursuers from being able to make the turn.

As the car started to turn, TJ raised his weapons and held the triggers. His body pushed against the car, and his arms swayed around. His aim became more inaccurate as his momentum almost made him fall out of the car. He only ceased firing when he saw the shattering of the windshield.

The van careened into a wall, demolishing the front of the vehicle. TJ felt relieved as Oden slowed the car before doing a U-turn in the middle of the road.

As they pulled up next to the van, TJ hopped out of the window and onto the ground. With his MP5 in hand, he cautiously approached. He looked and found the inside of the van to be a bloody mess. The driver was slumped against the wheel with multiple bullet holes through his chest. The passenger, it appeared, had died on impact as the van had shattered, sending debris into, and through, him. TJ opened the side door and looked in the back to see even more carnage.

A young man, who barely seemed twenty, lay in the back seat. The cushions and windows around him were still dripping with his blood.

There was however, one man in the vehicle who had survived. He stared up into TJ's eyes, unable to move. He looked even younger than the other man in the back. TJ could hear this one's breath as he struggled to continue breathing. TJ knew what he had to do.

He raised his gun and evened it with the young man's head. The man looked at TJ with pleading eyes as he began to whisper something.

TJ didn't give him the chance to finish. He pulled the trigger and a couple bullets entered the boy's head and ended his life.

"Okay, they're all dead," TJ said as he returned to the car.

"Good," Oden said. "Promise me one thing though. Next time you want to start acting like Rambo, at least warn me first."

TJ smiled before assuring him, "I doubt we'll have to worry about that any time soon. Let's get out of here." TJ implored as he once again climbed into the passenger seat.

"Do we have time to make the switch?" Davy asked.

"I was already planning on it" Oden responded.

"Do what?" TJ asked.

"Our good friends, the Israelis, were kind enough to hook us up with this car. But they also understood that something like this could happen.

124

"So we agreed on a location with them to use as a drop off point. They have two other vehicles there, same make, model, color, and year as what we're driving now. They check the location every few days and if we take a vehicle, their mechanics take our old one, refurbish and replace it, as good as new."

The men drove a few more miles before they eventually turned into a side gravel road. The road led to a closed gate.

Davy jumped out of the car and opened the gate. Once the car pulled through and he closed the gate behind them, he hopped back into the car. They searched for a few minutes before finding two identical vehicles parked next to a tree.

They parked on the opposite side of the tree from the other cars. Davy focused on cleaning up Yallsten as best he could so he wouldn't leave blood stains in the new vehicle. When they were finished tending to him, Oden began to examine the tree.

"Now, somewhere," His voice trailed off as he pulled out his knife. "Where is it?"

"What are you looking for?" TJ asked.

"Oh, there is a piece of a bark somewhere around here. It's artificial, and they've got it hidden pretty well. It's hiding a hollowed out part of the tree and on the inside of that is a set of keys and instructions. It's directions to a safe house, should our mission become compromised. I don't think that we should stay at the apartment any longer."

"Agreed", Yallsten moaned from the car.

"What will the bark look like?" TJ asked.

"Just run your hand over the tree until you find a piece that doesn't belong."

TJ put his hands on the tree and ran them across the bark, searching for anything that felt out of place.

"There we go! I found it!" Oden exclaimed.

TJ walked around to him and watched as Oden dug his pocketknife into the tree.

"TJ, come get this for me."

TJ walked over to Oden and helped him pull off the bark. Once it was in his hand Oden, reached inside and grabbed a car key. "TJ, you get the other stuff."

Oden rushed to the new car and opened the trunk. He pulled four separate bags out and tossed one to TJ before taking the other three to the car Yallsten was still sitting in.

"Clothes; they had our measurements. We want to be inconspicuous not be covered in blood."

TJ looked down at his shirt, which was speckled with blood from the man he had shot. He realized that it was a great plan and was impressed at how prepared the Israelis had been.

TJ clenched the key and paper in his hand and began to change.

Oden and Davy helped Yallsten undress then assisted him as he put the clean clothes on. Once Yallsten was taken care of, Davy and Oden changed their clothes and tossed the dirty, bloodied clothes into the car they were leaving behind.

The four men piled into the new car.

"Okay, TJ, tell us where they've got us staying," Oden requested.

"How about a resort on the beach? It's better than getting shot at." Yallsten joked.

TJ opened up the paper and read aloud. "The Leonardo Plaza Hotel Tiberias, 348."

"Well, Yallsten, it looks like you got your wish man!" Davy.

The men drove away and exited the area a different way than they had entered.

When they see that we took the key they'll contact us. When we get settled in, we'll have a lot of tedious work to do on our final plans."

"But," Davy interjected, "They want us to blend in, so maybe going down to the pool and relaxing wouldn't be a bad thing."

"Yes!" Yallsten excitedly agreed.

"Well, first and foremost we need to get our stuff done and stay hidden. Gunshot wounds to the leg are sadly not incognito." Oden said.

The sigh that came from the back seat meant that Yallsten understood. He would have to stay hidden in the room all day.

"I want us in and out of the building in less than twenty minutes," Oden challenged the men.

When they arrived at their apartment, they packed up their personal things and were gone in fewer than fifteen minutes. They knew that an Israeli forensic team would come through and get rid of any trace of them.

Chapter Twenty-Four

They parked at the side of the hotel, knowing that it would be less populated at that late hour of night. The men slipped in the door and carried Yallsten up the stairs. They wanted to remain unseen.

They opened the door to the room and slipped inside. Yallsten was the first to fall onto the bed.

"It's been too long since I've had a good night sleep or, a good bed," he sighed.

Davy shared the sentiment as he collapsed onto the other bed. "I hear you, brother. This is nice."

"You women, you don't see me or TJ whining about what beds we've had to put up with do you?" Oden harshly questioned before turning and looking at TJ, waiting for him to voice agreement.

"That's because I was home a few days ago," TJ sheepishly responded.

"Oh, in that case, move over Davy." He collapsed down onto the bed and let out a loud sigh as he relaxed.

Fifteen minutes later, the men were not talking about their plans or about what had happened before. Fifteen minutes later each of the men was sound asleep on his bed.

Yallsten woke up an hour later, unable to position himself comfortably because of his wound. As he slowly moved his leg, the bed bounced and shook. He looked to his side at TJ who was thrashing around. He knew that whatever TJ was dreaming about was not pleasant, so he painfully turned his body to face TJ and placed his hands on his shoulders to lightly shake him.

TJ jumped and gasped for air. His eyes were wide open as they darted back and forth.

"Holy crap man, you okay?" Yallsten whispered.

TJ took a few more deep breaths before answering. "Yeah, yeah, I'm fine."

"What exactly were you dreaming about? That seemed super intense."

"Oh, uh, I was dreaming about... hunting. Yeah, there was a, uh, a big buck, that I was hunting." TJ struggled as he continued. "It was just like, the thrill of the kill, you know? That's all."

"Man, I would have guessed it was you who was being hunted."

Yallsten figured he wouldn't get anything from TJ that TJ didn't want him to know, so he rolled onto his back once more, ready to sleep again. He closed his eyes, ignoring TJ's continued heavy breathing as he drifted off.

TJ knew Yallsten wasn't buying it. But he couldn't admit how bad his PTSD had gotten. Knowing he couldn't have another outburst like he had just had, TJ stood and rummaged through his bag in search of his pills. After he found them, he took a couple and walked into the bathroom to compose himself.

It took a few minutes, but TJ was eventually able to calm down enough to go back to bed.

At 9:45, Oden woke up and had to face the sad realization that he would not go back to sleep. He stood and walked to the bathroom, quietly shutting the door behind him. He began to shower and was unafraid and unashamed to try to use all the hot water the hotel had to offer.

Davy felt Oden get out of bed. He rolled over and sprawled out. He had no problem falling back asleep.

When Oden left the bathroom, TJ got up and hurried in to use the restroom, and shower. It took a few minutes before he was able to get the water temperature to a comfortable setting.

Pain coursed up through Yallsten's leg. He knew that being shot wasn't something that he would get used to instantly, but that didn't stop him from wishing.

He cringed in pain and threw off the bed covers. He looked at his leg before announcing, "I'm gonna need some new bandages, guys."

"Here you go," Oden said before tossing some to him.

Davy sat up, walked to the bathroom door. He heard the water running, knocked once, then walked in. He found an unused cup and began to fill it with water. As he walked out of the bathroom, he grabbed a washcloth and shut the door.

Yallsten watched as Davy carefully removed his bandages. He grimaced as Davy cleaned then redressed his wound. He knew that he could handle the pain; he just wanted to regain the ability to carry his weight.

Chapter Twenty-Five

TJ finished his shower and entered the room. He stood and watched as Davy finished with Yallsten before a knock on the door interrupted them all.

TJ looked at the others, silently asking permission to open the door.

Oden helped Davy cover Yallsten's leg before nodding to TJ.

TJ turned to the door and looked through it before opening it.

Outside, a man wearing a hotel uniform stood with two large bags on a cart. "Your luggage, sir."

TJ grabbed the bags off the cart, he struggled with their weight as he brought them into the room. He then shut the door, turned around. "What is it?" Oden asked.

"Don't know, but they sure are heavy," TJ said as he strained to lift the bags to the bed.

Oden opened the first bag and pulled out a laptop that he handed to Davy.

"Take care of this for us," he said before turning his attention back to the bags.

"Would you look at this?" Oden exclaimed.

He then proceeded to pull out package after package of ammunition. He handed them all to Yallsten who had excitedly sat up.

Oden picked up a small box and opened it. Inside the box sat individual blocks of C4.

"Oh boy," Yallsten whispered.

"I think we can have some fun with this," Oden said.

"I think they want us to hold off an army." TJ joked.

"That might actually be more accurate than you think," Davy said looking up from the laptop.

"What do you mean by that?" Oden demanded.

"We might be in for a bit more action then we thought we would be," Davy explained. "Look in the other bag. We should have a MK14 Mod 0 EBR rifle with a sniper scope on it."

"Oooh I want that." Yallsten said with a hint of jealousy.

"There also should be three M4A1 assault rifles and some more ammunition. All come equipped with silencers."

"What does this mean they want us to do?" Oden asked. He pulled out four M9 Beretta pistols and then four Molle Assault vests.

"Do they know Yallsten was shot?"

"That's what I'm trying to tell them. The terrorists knew that our informant was no longer with their cause so they sent some guys after him. Those were the guys that ended up chasing us, but we don't know how many were sent. If they got to the informant he might have told them we're looking at the camp. Which means we now have to strike fast to catch them before they disappear."

"Well, give us a rundown of what they have so far." Oden demanded.

"The Israelis and SEALs want to hit the base at sunrise. We'll split into two groups. The main fighting force will come down the mountains from the north. The secondary force will come in a van from the highway and set up an ambush to keep anyone from escaping down the hill. Now this is where things get interesting." Davy paused and looked at the men before continuing.

"The Israelis have identified a High Value Target. They want us to be part of two groups of three to go in after him. They want to get to the base as quickly and silently as possible and have us go in to grab the HVT."

"What about me?" Yallsten asked.

"I'm still working on it, but they are counting on us being fully operational."

"What if I use the MK?" Yallsten asked with a glimmer in his eye. "When we go in, we'll find a perch for me, and then I can help provide cover and identify the HVT."

"What makes you think you can make it up to a perch to do all that?" Oden asked.

"I've been through worse. I can climb, and I sure as hell know how to shoot!" Yallsten retorted.

Oden didn't like the idea of Yallsten having to make it up into a perch with his injury. He understood what could happen if Yallsten had to retreat, but he knew that the protection he could offer was worth the risk.

"Okay, Davy, see if they know of any perch we can get Yallsten into."

"Sure thing," Davy said before turning back to the computer to type. "With Alst shot, that'll change the plan a bit. Instead of him going in with us, we'll have one of the groups of three escort him to his perch and the other group of three waiting elsewhere.

"The camp is in the hills, as you all know. The main force is going to be working their way down the mountains. They somehow got a sketch of the patrol routes. There are guard towers at each corner, so we can sneak in before all the shooting starts and replace one of the camp guards with Yallsten."

"Before the shooting starts?" Oden asked.

"Whenever it starts, everyone in the camp will be on high alert. We won't have a chance to get him into the tower once the fighting begins because all their men will be scrambling. When Yallsten makes it into the tower, he can signal everyone that he's in place and ready, and then it begins."

"Okay. When will we get the whole thing planned out?"

"By the end of the night," Davy responded.

"What about the HVT?" Yallsten chimed in.

"Right now all I have is a name. Jasim. They're still working on getting intel on him."

"So we're gonna just go in blind and guess which guy to pick up?" TJ asked.

"No, they'll have sorted out." Davy explained before asking, "Hey, Alst can you toss me the notepad and pen from the desk? I'm gonna want to take some notes on what's going on."

"Sure," Yallsten replied. He opened the nightstand drawer and found a notepad and a pen and tossed them one by one to Davy.

The day passed as the men attempted to finalize their plans and relax whenever they could. They knew relaxation was not a commodity that would be offered to them in the next couple days. With that thought in mind, each of the men crawled into his bed and fell asleep.

Chapter Twenty-Six

He was running out of time. He had to make it to the top of the tower and fast. His leg, however, was slowing him down.

Davy was watching the path that they had just come by while Oden watched where the path led. Both were watching for enemy patrols. But they also knew that they were already behind schedule.

When the men had gotten into position they had radioed one of the SEALs. Suddenly there was a silenced shot and the man in the tower slumped to the bottom of the basket.

Yallsten was three-quarters of the way up. But anyone who looked at the tower would know that there was something wrong. The basket was empty. Yallsten had to replace the man and do it now.

Davy, Oden, and TJ knew another patrol would soon be approaching. They were exposed. They needed to retreat. Oden led the two other men into the brush. TJ turned around once again to check on Yallsten.

TJ watched as Yallsten was about to step into the tower. TJ didn't have a good feeling about the whole mission-it was all too quiet. TJ was sure someone in the camp would have looked up and noticed the switch being made.

TJ watched as Yallsten neared the basket. But as Yallsten was about to step into, the man in the basket jumped to his feet, surprising Yallsten. Yallsten jerked back in surprise. He landed on the rungs of the ladder, but his leg collapsed under his weight. His other leg stayed on the rung, and he caught himself before pulling himself back up.

The other man punched Yallsten. He absorbed the blow. TJ raised his weapon and aimed at the man. He stared down the holographic sight of his weapon. His breath steadied as his finger rested on the trigger. He knew that if he didn't hit his target right away Yallsten would soon fall to his death.

He pulled the trigger.

He saw the man grimace as the bullet hit him. The man dropped into the basket once more. Yallsten climbed in and pulled out his pistol. He shot the man twice then looked down and gave a thumbs up to the men below.

TJ turned and ran towards Oden and Davy. He saw that they were both kneeling behind a log and shooting towards the hill. TJ dove behind the cover of the log too.

"What's happening?" TJ asked.

"Enemy up the hill," Oden said between gunshots. "They started firing at us as we came back into the brush. It's like they were waiting for us."

"I have that C4," Davy said. "Cover me, and I'll toss some up there. When I get back, we play dead. Then as they start to approach we blow it."

"Do it quickly," Oden demanded. "Their gunfire is going to attract someone."

TJ stood up at the same time Oden did and they unleashed a fierce stream of bullets from their weapons. Oden shot in bursts with his rifle, trying to get as many hits as he could while TJ just sprayed bullets into the woods with his MP5.

Davy ran. He sprinted away from the gunfire and then turned up the hill and started putting the blocks of C4 on the ground. He heard the fire of the MP5 stop then start again moments later. He knew that Oden and TJ didn't have much time, and he had even less.

He gave up on putting the C4 down by hand and began tossing the blocks of explosives all over the hill. Davy sprinted back down and dove for cover behind the log. The three men stood up simultaneously and shot up the hill.

Each time there was a return of fire, one of the three men would not stand up again. After a few exchanges, all three Americans were on the ground, waiting.

Oden peeked over the log, and he could see the silhouettes of the terrorists coming closer. Oden turned to Davy and shook his head.

Davy held the detonator in his hand and waited.

Oden heard noise from the brush as the attackers neared.

"Now," he whispered.

The ground shook, and pieces of earth, bark from trees, and all other types of debris were soon raining over the log. The men stood up and shot at the few terrorists that had remained standing.

They continued up the hill to kill the last of them. TJ approached another who was lying on the ground. He looked down at the burnt and bloodied man and saw that he was still breathing. He pulled his gun out to end him right there as the man tried to speak. TJ didn't understand what had been said, so he aimed his gun at the man's head and fired.

The burst of blood that came from the man's head wasn't what had disturbed TJ. The man's uniform did. It looked familiar, and as he studied it he came to the realization that it was an Israeli Commando whom he had just shot.

TJ rushed over to the two other men and found that they had come to the same conclusion. Somehow one of the groups had gotten mixed up. Something had happened and one of them was at the wrong place.

TJ felt a sudden and intense tightness in his chest. He grabbed his chest and felt a warm flow of blood leaving his body. He dropped to his knees and looked up. While they were fighting their own people, a group of the terrorists had crept through the brush and surprised the remaining Americans.

Chapter Twenty-Seven

TJ held his hands over his chest. He didn't feel the bleeding anymore, but the tightness remained. He cautiously moved his hands away from his chest but was unable to spot the wound. TJ felt the bed below him move, so he instinctively looked to his side.

There Yallsten lay, eyes open looking at TJ.

"Morning," he said. "Sorry about that, I rolled on my leg wrong, and it made me jump."

"It's fine. I need to get up anyway," TJ replied.

TJ stood up and rolled off his bed. He walked to the bathroom and softly shut the door. TJ turned the water on in the shower then sighed as he sat down on the floor with his back against the door. He held his head in his hands as he sat there.

Yallsten stood up after hearing the water turn on, and in an attempt to grow accustomed to the pain began to pace from one side of the room to the other. He grimaced with each step but, because he knew he wouldn't be able to ignore the pain, he pushed on. He began to raise his legs quicker and quicker as if to run in place, grunting and moaning every time his foot hit the floor.

"What are you doing?" Oden asked while he sat on his bed watching Yallsten.

"Trying to get used to the pain," Yallsten answered.

Oden shook his head, and Davy laughed.

"Yeah, you have fun with that, Davy said. "I'm going to see what we know about the camp and the patrols."

Davy opened the laptop and began to type.

TJ then turned the water off and walked out of the bathroom. He joined the men as Davy was beginning to explain more about the camp.

"So it looks like there are a few different patrol routes. This makes it even more important that we get our timing right with Yallsten in the tower. The camp is built like a rectangle east to west. There is a guard tower about five feet outside the camp walls on each corner.

"The north side of the camp has multiple trees and a nice incline going up away from it. That is where the first force will be coming from.

"The east side of the camp is easily the most heavily wooded. We're not planning on doing much there. We hope the fighting lasts three to five minutes at the most. There shouldn't be a need to venture over that way.

"The south side is where we come from. The road leads up the mountain from the south and enters the camp. We'll keep anyone from escaping out the gates.

"The west side is where Yallsten will be in the tower, the southwest tower to be exact. It would be easier to put him in the north tower but, we think it would be better to keep him away from the fighting. Also, from the southwest side, he will be able to pick them off from behind.

"Now for the patrols. We think that there are two paths that the patrols will likely follow. We don't have a clue how many patrols are out at a time though. The first path comes out of the gate and down the road a ways before circling to the West around some trees. The patrols walk around the camp and stay close to the walls most of the way. On the east side, because the trees are so thick, we aren't sure where they go, but that's why we aren't doing anything there.

"The second patrol is odd. They don't have a path we can map out. They go on very unpredictable walks. They will go deep into the woods at some points only to reappear and hug the walls at other points."

"Why do we have the C4 then?" TJ asked.

"If we are able, we will put it down on the road at the entrance to the camp. If we can blow away enough of the road to make it impossible for a vehicle to drive through, then that makes it a lot harder for them to escape."

"So we just wait for the group in the north to kill everyone, then we go in and look for Jasim with them?" Oden asked.

"If everything works perfectly, then yes. We want him to be captured alive, but personally, I won't be too sad if he dies. But if a need arises for us to go into the camp, then we will be ready to do so."

"What do we have to deal with inside the camp in terms of resistance?" Oden asked.

"There has been increased traffic in and out of the camp within the past two days. Now whether that has something to do with your incident with the informant or something else entirely we don't know, but something is going on," Davy replied.

"They plan to toss six of us into the middle of what could be a hundred people?" TJ nervously asked.

"If the fighting breaks out, it will be in the north side, meaning that you will go in behind them. Stay in cover and don't shoot. Yallsten will be able to provide some cover fire, but you'll want to sprint around to the building Jasim is in."

"Well, I guess that works for me, Oden sighed.

Davy continued. "There are seven buildings in the camp. Three are barracks, and those are along the west wall. There is one that we believe to be an armory. It has a more western design and is near the north wall. It might have some extra people and weapons in it, so we want to be aware of what is coming out of there. There are two smaller buildings near the gate on the south side that we believe hold surplus weapons and food. Both are buildings that we wouldn't expect people to be in, but they are places someone could hide so, once again, be careful.

"Finally, on the east side is a much larger building. About two or three stories high, this is where their tactical stuff gets taken care of. It is also where we think Jasim will be. He will most likely have a few guys around him, and when a gunfight breaks out we don't know where he will retreat to. We don't want him to get comfortable. If we're going after him, once the attack starts, this is where we think he'll be headed."

"We will all have Bluetooth headsets that work as radios. Thank the Israelis for that. The group in the north will start on one frequency, and we'll be on another. Tabor will be sitting back with a couple of guys on computers, and they will make sure we know where our guys are so we don't shoot each other. When the north group makes it into the camp, Tabor will give them the okay and they will switch to our frequency and do what they can to help us."

Now that the plan was solidified, the men ordered room service. As they ate, they watched TV and talked to each other about home. An undeniable tension had been building in the room for the last twenty-four hours. It had started when they received the bags filled with their weapons and had only grown as they discussed the plan. They knew they were in for something big, but they wouldn't know how intense it would be until the next morning.

Chapter Twenty-Eight

Each knew the seriousness of the situation they would soon be facing. They stepped out of the plane to meet the Israelis and SEALs who had been waiting for them.

Yallsten had convinced the men that his leg was good enough for him to make it up the ladder, but he wasn't sure. He knew that he and his leg would be holding the weight of everyone's lives as he made the climb. In less than eight hours he would find out just what his leg was capable of.

Oden made sure to tell the men that he wanted to be in the group that was taking Yallsten to the guard tower. He then volunteered to take the two men, who weren't with the CIA, with him for the attack. Oden also claimed the C4 for his squad so that the second could focus on capturing Jasim.

TJ and Davy agreed, even though they weren't fond of splitting their team they knew that Oden's replacement would undoubtedly be just as capable.

Moments later a large van pulled in and parked beside them. In the driver's seat sat David Tabor.

Tabor climbed out of the van and approached the men. They greeted each other with a handshake before Oden pulled Tabor aside to make sure that he would be taking Yallsten to the guard tower. Tabor nodded in understanding. They continued talking for a few moments then joined the other three men.

Davy and TJ had sorted out the weapons and ammo while the two leaders were talking. Each weapon had a silencer, and the men all had an equal amount of ammunition.

The four men then climbed into the full van while Tabor reclaimed his seat behind the wheel.

"Cantor, Bassano, the two of you are going with Oden and Yallsten. Make sure he makes it into the tower safely. After that you will follow Oden through the camp."

Two Israeli men in the back of the van nodded in agreement.

"Mitchell, you will join your American counterparts. You, Davy, and TJ will enter the camp as soon as an opening appears. Once you get in, be quick, but don't be reckless. I don't care which one of you takes the lead, so you all can figure that out."

A young blonde man behind TJ and Davy spoke up and introduced himself as Caleb Mitchell. TJ and Davy both introduced themselves as Tabor continued to address the group.

They drove for an hour taking obscure side roads which had less traffic. When they reached the border, Tabor turned and reminded the men that if the border guard decided he didn't want the money he had been offered, they would kill him as silently as possible and hide his body before moving on.

TJ didn't like the idea of just blowing away a guard because he was in the wrong place at the wrong time, but he knew they needed to do whatever it took to get into the camp. He just hoped the guard would be smart enough to accept the bribe so he wouldn't end up rotting in some bush.

Tabor rolled the window down and talked quietly with a guard who had stopped them before passing him an envelope and driving on.

"Okay, men, we're clear."

"How much did you have to shell out to him?" Oden growled.

"Nothing of ours," Tabor said. "We confiscate guns and drugs and such, then sell it on the black market, bust the guys we sell it to, and repeat the process. We've been able to pay for a few operations, give a couple bonuses, and develop a nice surplus that way. America should try it sometime. You might relieve some of that crushing debt."

"Well, we tried something similar, but a bunch of Americans got killed and we ended up supplying weapons to the drug cartel."

"Oh yes, I forgot your government isn't responsible."

"Never has been. You should try working for them."

"I'd rather avoid that."

Most of the men in the back of the van found humor in the banter between the two leaders and laughed. It was a great moment that relieved a lot of the tension that had filled the van as they had approached the border.

Tabor pulled the van off the road. After parking he explained, "We will have to wait here about thirty minutes before moving into our final position."

He then pulled out a piece of paper and handed it to the four men who had joined them.

"This is a picture of Jasim."

TJ studied the photo, trying to find something about the man that would make him stand out. As he scanned the picture a second time, he was shocked to find something that was unique about him: his eyes were the color of emerald.

"Green eyes? That isn't common is it?"

"No," Tabor said. "His mother was from England. She visited Iran for studies for her university but somehow ended up staying with a group of people that taught her to hate all things Israeli and Western. She passed her green eyes on to her son. She then helped raise him to hate our cultures as well. Our intelligence community had monitored her, but she stayed with the extremists willingly, so there was nothing for us to do. She eventually just disappeared. We assume that she did something to make her husband angry and then he got rid of her."

"How could he do that?" TJ wondered aloud.

"Probably with a gun or a blade," Tabor answered.

"No, not her husband- Jasim. How could he be a part of this crusade against the west if they had done that to his own mother? Surely he knows what happened to her. It just seems so..."

"Unnatural?" Oden suggested.

"Yeah, that's it." TJ agreed.

He didn't understand the heartlessness that permeated from this "religion of peace." He knew that each set of beliefs, ranging from atheism to Christianity to Islam all had people who would claim those beliefs and then taint them with their actions. But strangely enough, TJ found that those who were the most extreme followers of Islam were the violent ones he was fighting against.

Tabor turned back around and said, "Okay, men, it's time."

That was all Tabor needed to say. The men in the van all stirred from their relaxed positions as the van began to move. They traveled east on the main road, no longer trying to remain concealed.

By now the SEALs and Commandos of the first group would have about two miles left in their hike to the camp. They would take up their positions once they arrived, and then they would wait.

The van turned and slowly started to climb up a mountain.

"This road takes us to the camp. Be ready. Assume everyone and everything you see is hostile."

TJ had never heard of, or participated in, an operation with such loose of rules of engagement. But he knew, should anything go wrong, all blame would be on the Israelis, so they had the right to pick their own set of rules.

Tabor's words also served to reaffirm something all the men had already understood. They were in hostile territory and under no circumstance would any of them receive the benefit of the doubt.

Chapter Twenty-Nine

TJ, Davy, and Mitchell walked through the woods and up an incline to their position. They could barely make out a small light in the sky, and they knew it was from the guard tower. They had exited the van thirty minutes ago; five minutes after Oden led his group away.

Oden's voice crackled from the radio. "In position."

TJ didn't know how far away from the tower the other group was, but he assumed they were much closer to their tower than he was to his. The need to move quickly would demand that Yallsten be close to the tower.

"Give us a second; we're almost there," Davy whispered in reply.

The three men all had their weapons in hand, ready to shoot if necessary to keep their arrival secret. Davy led the way with TJ in the middle and Mitchell following four feet behind. Two minutes later they were in position.

They found a tree that had fallen and sat on it.

"In position," Mitchell whispered.

"Good. Any word from Tabor about the other group?" Oden responded.

"No, we haven't heard anything about them," Mitchell replied.

"Okay. Remember: no news is good news. Radio silence from now on unless it's an emergency," Oden commanded.

TJ looked at Mitchell and Davy, who nodded in response. TJ watched as an occasional shadow blocked the small glowing orb of light they saw in the sky. TJ knew it was just the guard moving around, but everything he saw made him even more anxious than he already was.

A faint voice caught TJ's attention and he turned to his side to see Mitchell leaned forward, whispering. TJ watched until Mitchell sat upright before asking, "What was that?"

"Oh, I was just praying."

"Praying?"

"Yeah, I do it before all of my operations. And I guess it works, because I haven't died yet."

"Well," TJ said, "I hope it works for all of us."

TJ looked up through the dry leaves into the sky. He could already tell that sunrise was nearing. The sky had turned a lighter shade and, he knew that in moments their operation would be in full swing. His heart pounded in anticipation.

He looked back at the other men. Mitchell seemed to be admiring the heavens as well. Davy, however, was sitting perfectly still with his eyes closed. TJ didn't think he was asleep, although he would have been impressed if any man had been able to fall asleep knowing what would soon happen. He saw no reason to shake Davy out of his trance, so he looked back into the sky and waited.

TJ began to think about Emy. He was ready to be home so he could be around her again. He hoped that the next time he was home it would be for more than a few days. He thought of her radiant smile but was interrupted by Mitchell's voice.

"It's a girl, isn't it?"

"What?" TJ asked.

"It's a girl. No one smiles like you were just smiling before a mission like this if he isn't thinking of a girl."

"Oh, yeah, it is. My wife Emy. She's beautiful and has the best personality you could imagine. Kindest person you could ever meet. What about you? You have a wife?"

"Yeah. You just described her perfectly. Except her name isn't Emy- it's Millie. A smile that never leaves her face. I've seen her in the worst of times, and that smile is still there."

"Really?"

"Yeah, when she was diagnosed with cancer, she responded with a smile and a laugh instead of cowering from it. The smile is always there, but even more impressive is that its genuine at all times. Happy no matter what life throws at her."

"Wow. She sounds pretty amazing. I really hope she beats the cancer. Sorry you guys have to deal with it."

"Me too. You wouldn't know she had cancer unless she took the wig off. That wig is the only fake thing on her head. Her smile is real."

The two men continued to share this glimpse into the life of the other until Oden interrupted them on the radio.

"Okay, we're starting now. Moving Yallsten into position."

The Israeli commandos escorted Yallsten closer to the tower. Oden was sitting back fifty yards with his rifle trained on the guard in the tower. Oden would have to wait for Yallsten to get on the ladder before he could take the shot. It was a bad angle but the best he could get.

Yallsten placed his hands on the rungs and began to climb. He was as silent as he could be, but the ladder creaked under his weight. He tried to move carefully to prevent himself from making any more noise, but he couldn't stop. He had to keep climbing.

Oden watched as the man in the tower became aware of Yallsten's presence. Yallsten was nearing the basket, and the guard knew someone was climbing. Judging by the man's laugh he expected a friend. Oden watched as the man in the basket's smile turned to a look of surprise.

Oden steadied himself, exhaled, and squeezed the trigger. The man fell back into the basket.

At the moment the guard began to realize what was happening, he saw the stranger aim a pistol at him. He tried to yell to warn the others, but as two bullets tore through his chest he didn't have enough life left to make a noise.

"I'm in position." Yallsten whispered.

"Good. We're moving back now," Oden replied. The two Israeli men rushed to join Oden, and then the three men crept back into the brush. They were, once again, hidden from everyone at the camp. The sky was becoming illuminated by the sun. Yallsten could now look through his scope and see any of the other men in the towers. But that meant they could see him as well.

"I see your man on the southeast tower," Yallsten told TJ, Davy, and Mitchell. "Want me to take him out for you and loosen things up over there?"

Mitchell looked at Davy and shook his head.

"Not now. We don't know where the patrols are, and he won't be able to do much when the attack starts. Save him for later."

"Okay. I have to wait a few more minutes before signaling the first group. I can't see the north wall, I need more light."

"It's your call." Oden told him. "We can wait a bit longer."

"We're ready whenever you're good to go." Davy assured him.

"The camp seems pretty lifeless. Who knows? Maybe we'll get lucky and catch them all sleeping. Oh, hang on! Wait a second. Yeah, Oden I see a patrol coming to me. Can you guys take care of them?"

"Where are they?"

"About eighty yards away, 2 o'clock right now."

"We'll be ready for them."

Oden and the two Israelis sank down and waited for the patrol to come. There were two men approaching.

"I'll take the closest one. Both of you hit the farthest guy. On three."

Oden raised his weapon.

"One."

He breathed in softly and centered his sight right under his target's neck.

"Two."

He followed the man with his rifle.

"Three."

He gently pulled the trigger. The gun recoiled against his shoulder. His target fell to the ground, clutching his throat. The other man fell face first into the dirt as two bullets ripped into his chest.

"They're down."

Oden and the Israelis approached the two men and made sure they were dead before dragging their bodies into the woods and concealing them in the brush.

"I'm about to make the call. Everyone ready?" Yallsten asked.

"We're good," Mitchell whispered.

"Good," Oden replied.

Yallsten contacted Tabor and made sure the attacking force was ready. He explained to them who he wanted the first group to take out and when.

Tabor wished him luck then relayed the message to the first team.

Yallsten contacted the two groups of three that were on his side and spoke to them. "I told the first group we're ready. Once I see the two opposite guards are taken care of I'll, tell you, and then you all move into the camp. I'll take out the remaining guard and you'll be clear."

Chapter Thirty

Yallsten saw a red mist burst out of the northeast guard's head. Then he looked to his left and found that guard had already slumped down into the basket.

"Two guards down," he said.

Yallsten raised his gun and looked down the scope to the east tower. He saw the guard fumbling with his weapon as he attempted to figure out what had just happened to the other two sentries. Yallsten knew the man would soon try to raise the alarm.

The man did just that. He picked something up- Yallsten couldn't see what it was. Maybe a radio? Whatever it was, it meant that he didn't have much time. He hurriedly aimed the sight at the man and fired. The bullet made contact with the man's arm, and he dropped his gun and the electronic device.

Yallsten now had the time he needed in order to get a better shot. He peered through the scope and waited for the man to peek back over the basket. Once he did, Yallsten pulled the trigger and sent a bullet tearing through the man's skull.

"I got him. You're clear."

"We heard the impact," Mitchell said.

Yallsten heard a burst of gunfire erupt from the north side of the camp. He looked through his scope and saw that two of the terrorists had figured out that there were men in the woods. They were now wildly shooting their guns hoping, to hit someone.

Even though they were too inaccurate to do damage, the noise from their guns and the attention that it would draw would be worse.

Both of the men fell to the ground. Yallsten had seen a couple of bursts from the woods that he assumed had killed them.

But what he saw now was much more frightening.

"Crap! We've got guys pouring out of the barracks!" he screamed.

"Let the first group take care of it, and we'll sneak in and grab Jasim. Everything according to plan. Davy, lead your group in first and we'll follow you," Oden commanded.

"On our way," Davy said.

Davy, Mitchell, and TJ had been moving to the gate once the guard nearest them had been taken down. They paused outside the gate.

"We clear to go in?" Davy asked.

"Yeah, turn the corner and get behind that first building quickly," Yallsten ordered.

Davy led the two other men inside, and they sprinted to the building.

"Hold there!" Yallsten commanded.

Davy, Mitchell, and TJ did as they were told and stopped behind the building.

"Some guys just turned around. I think they're eyeing an escape," Yallsten said.

He watched as the men momentarily looked back at the gate then turned to continue fighting. A man carrying a RPG ran from the building that intel had identified as armory. He raised and fired the weapon into the woods.

A fiery explosion shook the ground and damaged the fence, knocking a small section of it down.

"What was that?" Davy and Oden simultaneously asked.

"A RPG, A guy shot it into the woods. Just knocked part of the fence down and now there are trees and large sections of the fence on fire."

"Fire? How wooded is the area that group one is in?" Oden demanded.

"Very... why?"

At that moment, he realized that he didn't need to ask. He saw the fire jump from the fence to other trees. As the flames began to spread from tree to tree, he knew what would happen. The first group would have to escape the fire by pouring into the camp through the missing wall. When they did, they would all be killed. They were being funneled to their deaths.

Yallsten raised his rifle and began to shoot at the men surrounding the missing wall. He knew that by exposing his position he would be putting himself in grave danger, but he had to relieve the pressure on the first group.

After he killed a couple enemies, other terrorists began to figure out what was happening. Some of the men turned around and began to fire at the tower. Yallsten ducked into the basket and called for help.

"I need help now. I'm pinned down in the tower, and our men are running right into an ambush! Tabor, we need all of you up here at the camp now!"

"Should we engage?" Davy asked.

"Negative. They still don't know you're there. We will engage. You guys grab Jasim," Oden commanded.

The men in the van all jumped out and sprinted up the hill. They knew that every second that it took to climb the hill could prove costly for their men.

"I'm not taking this C4 in with me," Oden said.

He put the C4 container down between the gate and the tower. He and the two Israeli men continued sprinting to the gate. When they got there, they paused.

"You guys need to be running now. Once we draw attention to us, you won't have a chance." Oden said.

The three men hiding behind the storage building looked at each other, then sprinted.

Chapter Thirty-One

TJ ran alongside the wall. They were thirty-five yards away from the storage building. They had heard the gunfire behind them and were happy they weren't near it. As they ran towards the building, they hoped to find Jasim.

Then they heard Yallsten's voice. "Thanks, guys. I'm as clear as I'm going to be. I couldn't stay up there. I'll try to provide cover at the gate. Tell me when you're coming out."

Mitchell, Davy, and TJ all collapsed against the building. In a few seconds they had caught their breath and were, again, moving along the wall.

Mitchell turned to Davy and TJ. "We have to make this quick. I don't know if you saw those flames, but they're spreading fast. I don't want to be stuck here when everything is on fire."

"A forest fire and a couple gunfights all around us, all part of a balanced breakfast," Davy joked.

The men chuckled then tiptoed along the wall hoping, to find a door. Twenty feet later, they found and gathered around one.

Davy and TJ stood on each side of the door and Mitchell stood in front of it. He raised his foot and kicked it in. Davy and TJ both turned into the doorway, ready to shoot should anyone be there.

Chapter Thirty-Two

Oden shot. He just wanted to provide some cover fire for Yallsten. He wasn't going to let him die. He couldn't.

Bullets whizzed by, forcing him and the Israelis into cover. As they dove behind what little cover they could find, they heard more shots from behind them. Oden turned to see that Tabor and his men had made it to the gate. He turned back and finished firing his magazine at the terrorists.

He heard Yallsten over the radio. "Thanks guys, I'm as clear as I'm going to be. I couldn't stay up there. I'll try to provide cover at the gate. Tell me when you're coming out."

"Thank goodness." Oden thought to himself. He knew TJ and Davy were on their own and were still very much in harm's way. But he had made sure one of his men was safe. At the moment, that was all he could ask for.

Chapter Thirty-Three

The men stared down each side of the hallway, TJ to the left and Mitchell to the right.

"Which way are we going?" Davy asked.

"No idea. Which way do you want?" Mitchell responded.

"Let's go right. We came from the left on the outside. This hallway is on the edge of the building, so we would probably have heard anything inside. Plus, we can't split up."

"Okay. Let's go," Mitchell said.

They carefully walked down the hall, stopping at each room to clear it and check for Jasim. But they didn't have to fire their guns, they found no one. The building seemed completely abandoned. They continued to creep down the hallway, listening for any sign of life other than themselves, but there was none. They approached the end of the hall and walked through a doorway which led to an abandoned stairwell.

"Up or down?" TJ asked.

"Down. Anyone who was up would have already tried to come down when the fighting started. There isn't another exit up top. People underground might not have noticed what's happening outside," Mitchell said.

"Good thinking. We'll follow you," Davy said.

Chapter Thirty-Four

Yallsten picked up the C4. He had an idea.

He ran as fast as his injured leg would carry him. He passed the tower and rounded the corner. When he stopped, he armed the C4 and kept them all in the container. He heard the gunfire mere feet away, but he knew the enemy wasn't aware of his presence yet.

He slung the C4 as far over the wall as he could, then ran another thirty feet away and dove into some brush. He got his rifle ready then pulled the detonator out and clicked it.

The explosion shook the ground and more fire filled the sky. Debris rained over him.

He aimed and began to shoot the men that he could see.

"That was me," Yallsten explained into his headset. "I won't be able to stay in this position for long, but they're surrounded while I'm here."

Chapter Thirty-Five

Oden heard the click of his gun and immediately dropped to his knees behind cover. He had to reload and do it quickly. There were three men coming around the building that he had to hold back.

Suddenly a blast shook the ground, and he heard screams from around the corner. He peeked around the building and saw that there was now a hole in the west wall.

He then heard Yallsten's voice confirm what he had suspected. "That was me. I won't be able to stay in this position for long but they're surrounded while I'm here."

"Well, you just saved my life. If there was anyone else in that part of the barracks you, took care of them too. You did good, Yalst. Thanks."

Chapter Thirty-Six

As the men glided down the stairs, the ground shook. The three men paused in their tracks.

"What just happened?" Davy whispered.

"No idea," Mitchell responded.

TJ shook his head and shared the same bewildered look as the other two. Then their radio crackled.

"That was me. I won't be able to stay in this position for long, but they're surrounded while I'm here,"

"Well, we know what that was now." Davy whispered.

The radio then crackled again. "Well, you just saved my life. If there was anyone else in that part of the barracks you took care of them too. You did good, Yalst. Thanks."

The men entered an identical hallway.

Mitchell led the way once again, and they checked the first two rooms they came to. As they were exiting the second room, shots rang out from farther down the hall.

Mitchell jumped back into the room pushing, TJ and Davy inside.

"Two shooters," Mitchell whispered.

He stood inside the doorway with Davy right behind him. Mitchell dropped to his knee and leaned out the door. Once he was crouched, Davy leaned out and over him. Both men fired twice and dropped their man with surgical precision.

They continued on, made it to the end of the hall, and verified that neither of the men was Jasim.

They stepped over the bodies and looked into the room the dead men had come from. TJ silently crept into the room with his weapon raised. He was ready to blow away anyone he saw in the room. As he took another step, he heard movement to his left. He turned just in time to catch a bar across his temple. TJ collapsed to the floor, fighting to stay conscious. He heard a scuffle, then the distinct sound of gunshots. A body fell next to TJ. He didn't know whether it was Davy's, Mitchell's, or the enemy's.

His question was soon answered as he saw a shadow reach down and grab his arm, before Mitchell helped him to his feet.

TJ saw Mitchell's mouth open and recognize he was trying to say something, but the ringing in his ears kept him from hearing what was said. He nodded to Mitchell then toward the hallway to make sure they knew he was good to go. They entered it again and continued down the corridor.

There were two more rooms before the end of the hallway. The doors were even with each other on opposite sides. The men would have to clear both rooms simultaneously.

"No surprises, guys. We check them both at the same time," Mitchell said.

"TJ, you take the left side, I'll take the right. Mitchell, cover us," Davy commanded. TJ was happy to at least be able to hear what Davy had said. The ringing in his head was subsiding but hadn't stopped. He knew he would have to fight this raging headache while finishing the mission.

Mitchell nodded and stepped forward with his gun ready. Davy and TJ cautiously and simultaneously approached the doors. Both paused, looked at each other, nodded, then breached the rooms.

Chapter Thirty-Seven

"Where are you guys? We need to be getting out of here. We can't find Jasim. He must have made it out before we got here. Where are you?" Oden pleaded.

The fire was raging and threatening to consume the camp. The east wall would be engulfed in flames in a few minutes. They didn't have long. Four of the men from the first group had been shot. Another 3 were hurt by the RPG explosion. They were able to make it down the hill to a vehicle that was waiting for them.

The three Americans, however, were still unaccounted for.

A couple of the terrorists were still alive and fighting, but they posed little threat to the wounded who were being evacuated. The rest of the men, who were sweeping through the camp, were trying to find TJ, Davy, and Mitchell.

Yallsten had to move from the west wall but was able to find a new cover and take out the remaining enemies.

Oden tried to raise the missing three on the radio again. "Where are you? Stay on this frequency. We have to retreat down the hill because of the fire. My God, you'd better be okay."

Chapter Thirty-Eight

Both men leaned into the doorway, saw a man, and shot.

Mitchell heard the exchange of fire. The man on his right, Davy, fell to the floor, but the one to his left remained standing. Mitchell jumped into the doorway and finished off the wounded man in the room.

TJ had killed his man but turned to find Davy lying on the ground.

"Oh, man! Davy, are you okay?" TJ yelled.

"Uh," Davy grunted. "Yeah. I'll be good. The vest took the worst of it for me. Just help me up."

Mitchell helped Davy to his feet then put Davy's arm around his shoulder and helped him walk to the end of the hall.

Their radios began to buzz with static.

"Anyone catch that?" Mitchell asked.

"No, I didn't understand any of it." TJ said.

"No," Davy moaned.

"What do we do?" TJ asked.

"Finish the mission. It's the only thing we can do," Mitchell said before he turned to Davy.

"You good?" he asked.

"No, I'm having some issues breathing. I'm gonna slow us down some."

"That's fine," TJ said.

"Lead the way, TJ," Mitchell commanded.

The men soon found another staircase. Unlike the others this one only led down. TJ made it to the bottom and checked the area while Mitchell and Davy struggled to get down the stairs.

They stepped forward and walked towards the only opening they could see. The opening they had found led them into a cave in the mountain.

There were two large caverns that they could go through. As the men looked into the entrances, trying to figure out which way to go, gunfire erupted from the one on the right. The three men returned fire with pinpoint accuracy and dropped the four men ahead of them in the cave.

As they continued, they were met with more gunfire. Davy collapsed to the ground, still struggling to catch his breath. Mitchell glanced at him momentarily before returning fire. He then commanded TJ to go along the wall and flank them.

TJ stayed low and moved as Mitchell shot back at the terrorists. TJ had left his rifle with Davy and now ran holding his pistol. It was much easier to maneuver, and he knew that if he wasn't as quick as possible, he would be killed.

TJ found a small pathway that led down and behind the men shooting at Mitchell. He followed it, stepping softly so he wouldn't make the enemy aware of his presence.

As he rounded the corner, he raised his pistol. There were four more men here, all shooting at Mitchell. Their bullets chipped away at the rocky cover hiding Mitchell and Davy.

TJ raised his pistol and began to shoot. He shot once at the first man, and twice at the rest. But his first shot alerted the other four to his presence.

The first man died instantly.

The second man was shot in the back and side of the head as he had turned to face TJ.

The third man was shot twice in the chest. Both bullets had entered him after he had turned around but before he could fire.

The fourth man dove to the side and out of TJ's sight as he was fired upon. He groaned in pain as a bullet grazed him.

TJ frantically tried to reload his weapon but was soon knocked to the ground by another man.

He looked up and saw two men. One had blood running down his arm. TJ instantly noticed his green eyes. The other man, who seemed to be unscathed, picked TJ up off the ground and slammed him into the wall.

The full force of TJ's body hit the wall causing, him to slump to the floor again.

The man grabbed TJ and held him up as Jasim staggered towards him.

"Any friends or family you have are going to die," he whispered calmly. He turned to the other man "Kill him, but make sure he feels it."

TJ tried to keep an eye on Jasim, but as the other man's fist connected with his face, he lost sight of him. TJ then lurched forward as the man's fist made contact with his stomach.

"Stop right now!" Mitchell yelled.

TJ was relieved to see that Mitchell had come to his aid. But as his body was spun around, he knew there wasn't much Mitchell would be able to do.

TJ felt the barrel of a gun press against his head as the man behind him positioned TJ between himself and Mitchell's gun.

TJ was still trying to recover from smashing into the wall. He felt like dead weight. His legs were weak. He could only stand because he was being held up by the man beating him.

"Stop now or I shoot," Mitchell coolly commanded.

TJ felt the breath of the man as it flowed against his ear. He didn't think Mitchell had a shot.

He then felt a warm splash on the back of his head, and suddenly he and the man were both falling to the floor. He reached behind himself to find that, not only had Mitchell had a shot, but he had taken it.

Chapter Thirty-Nine

TJ lay on the ground, trying to regain his composure. Davy and Mitchell were now standing over him; both offered him a hand to help him up.

"You okay?" Mitchell asked.

"Yeah, I'm fine. Nice shot."

They walked for a hundred yards before seeing a small glimmer of sunlight in the distance. They exited the cave and looked up at the fiery sky above them.

"Oden, where are you?" TJ yelled into his headset.

"Where have you guys been? We had to get away from that blaze. Please don't tell me you're stuck in the camp."

"No. We went into that building and found a few stairways that took us into a cave. We just now exited the mountain. We didn't find Jasim though. We'll try to find the road and come down to you." Mitchell said.

"We'll keep an eye out for you."

When the men found the others, they entered the vehicle and recapped what had happened. Tabor drove down the road and away from the blaze, but the whole time TJ had to deal with the knowledge that he had let Jasim get away.

The terrorist not only got away, but did so after threatening TJ's family. TJ didn't think Jasmin had the resources to find out anything about him or his family. But knowing that he had made the threat and then escaped was still unnerving. TJ had to protect Emy, no matter the cost.

Chapter Forty

Emy waited in the car for TJ. He had just landed and soon they would be reunited.

TJ walked out of the airport with a bag in his hand. He was relieved that this bag held clothes and civilian items instead of guns and C4.

He kept his personal gun on him in case Jasim tried to make good on his threat.

The whole time TJ was traveling back home he had wondered whether he should quit and try to move his family or stay in Des Moines. He didn't want to force Emy to quit her job. He did, however, come to the conclusion that it was time to retire. He didn't want to risk having to leave again and taking the chance that Jasim would hunt her down while he was gone.

He saw the car and approached it. After tossing his bags into the trunk, he opened the passenger door and sat down. He kissed his wife and began to talk to her as she pulled the car out.

As he spoke, he looked out the windows. He felt his heart sink and his stomach tighten. Outside the car TJ saw a familiar pair of green eyes watching. The man with those eyes was standing on the sidewalk as TJ and Emy drove past him. The eyes were locked on TJ's car and its driver. Jasim had seen TJ kiss the woman in the car, and now Jasim knew exactly who to target. TJ instantly paled and was silent.

"You okay babe?"

"Yeah." He struggled. "I'm just tired. No big deal."

"Let's get you home."

"I have something to tell you, Emy."

"What?" she asked, with a hint of concern in her voice.

"I think I'm going to retire."

Emy smiled, "That's great!" she exclaimed. She tried to smile, but she knew something was off. TJ wouldn't retire, at least without discussing it with her first. She sensed that something must have gone very wrong to make him feel this way.

TJ knew how happy the news had made her, but he could see some reservation in her eyes.

He had decided he wouldn't tell her about Jasim. Not yet, at least. He now knew that they would have to move. Seeing Jasim at the airport gave him no other option. He was trying to make sure that they weren't being followed home, but he knew that if they stayed in Des Moines, Jasim would find them.

They pulled into their apartment and TJ exited the car and scanned the surroundings. He knew that to Emy he would appear paranoid, but paranoia might be the only thing that could keep both him and Emy alive.

After they had unpacked the car and entered the home, they sat down on the couch. Emy confronted him. "TJ, something is bothering you. What's wrong?"

TJ sighed. He didn't want to admit his failure but he knew she needed to know.

"There was a guy that we were after. A really evil man named Jasim. We had six men and, we were supposed to go in and capture him. Some stuff happened, and we got split up. I ended up by myself. I shot him in the arm but someone else attacked me. After that guy knocked me to the ground, Jasim had him pause for a moment and then came over and told me that he was going to find my family and kill them. Kill you. He got away."

"And you think he's coming here?" Emy gasped in horror.

"I'm think he's already here and that he's coming after you because of me," TJ admitted.

"But how would he know where to find us? He didn't even know who you are. You just got back. There is no way that he beat you here. You're just being paranoid TJ, he can't be here." Emy assured him.

"If he has the resources, he could be. He's smart enough to find a way in undetected. He can move around completely unnoticed. I think," TJ stuttered, "I think we need to move."

"There's got to be another way. Let's call the police for help. Or can't you call the people you work for? We can't give up everything and move just because he threatened us," Emy began to cry. "Where will we go?"

"I don't know. I think we should get away from everything. Get a cabin in the mountains somewhere- you know, like the one we went to on our honeymoon."

"You want us to go and live like hermits? Leave everything we know and just abandon family and friends just to go live in the mountains? Away from everyone? Give me a location, TJ." she demanded.

"I don't know. Something like Montana or Wyoming?"

Emy continued crying as TJ put his arms around her and apologized.

"When should we leave?" she sobbed.

"As soon as possible."

"What are we supposed to do?"

"Just start over together, I guess. I'm so sorry, Emy," he whispered.

"It's okay," she whimpered. "It's not your fault."

TJ cringed as he heard her words. He knew her pain was his fault. He knew he was the one that had let Jasim get away, and he was the reason she was in danger now. If he had just done his job correctly, she wouldn't have to deal with this.

Emy excused herself, stood, and walked to the bathroom. She wanted to be alone and to calm down.

TJ watched Emy enter the bathroom. He was drained. He knew anyone coming into the apartment would awaken him, so he allowed himself to drift to sleep.

Chapter Forty-One

TJ opened his eyes as Emy stepped out of the bathroom. He watched her walk towards him with the wooden walls of their cabin in the background.

They were happy and safe now. It had all worked out fine. They had moved from Des Moines to Montana and now lived in a small secluded cabin.

They had to adjust to living in the country. They took up hunting together, and just over a week ago they had killed their first buck. Emy spotted it, and TJ had killed it with one shot.

They had wanted to mount the head and display it in their home. But the deer had decomposed quickly. They had to settle. They would mount the head on their wall but without the skin. Just the bones. The eye sockets seemed to gaze, at them and follow them wherever they went. It was creepy, but they had gotten used to it.

They were happy now, and that was all that mattered.

Emy sat down on the couch next to TJ. He put his arm around her. He looked at the hallway she had just come from. His dream and the illusion of happiness it had created left as Emy whispered, "I'm scared. I don't want to leave."

"I know, Emy. I'm sorry."

"Let's go to bed. We can sleep on it and then make a decision tomorrow morning over breakfast," Emy pleaded, even though she knew the decision was already made.

"That's a great idea," he whispered.

For a short time they lay in bed talking, before Emy fell asleep. TJ watched his wife sleep and was once again amazed at how beautiful she was. He kissed her forehead before falling asleep.

TJ woke up in the middle of the night as Emy left the bed to go to the restroom, as he watched her leave the room he fell back asleep. TJ heard a muffled noise. He stood and walked into the hallway and saw that the living room lights were on. He walked into the room and was horrified by what he saw.

Emy lay on the floor covered in blood. She wore a pair of shorts and a t-shirt that was torn apart at the bottom. Her stomach had been cut open, but her chest was still slowly rising and falling.

TJ was enraged as he looked to Emy. He dropped to his knees beside her.

Jasim had found her. Even at home, TJ hadn't been able to protect her. He had failed again, and it would cost Emy her life.

He cried, beside her and begged her to forgive him. He apologized as he wept, but she was unresponsive. The energy that it was taking her to breathe was draining the life from her body.

The only thing TJ could do at the moment was to watch Emy as she died, and he knew that was exactly what Jasim had wanted.

He looked into her eyes "I'm sorry. I'm so sorry Emy. Please forgive me."

Emy stared into her husband's eyes as she drew one final breath. She didn't have the strength to smile, or to tell TJ she didn't blame him or that he would be okay without her. She died in his arms unable to say any of the things she wanted him to know. She was unable to let him know that she forgave him and that she didn't blame him.

TJ fell next to Emy and put his arms around her as he wept. There was nothing he could say and nothing he could do to make this right. He had failed the most important person in his life. He sobbed as he kissed her forehead and held her hand.

She was gone.

He knew that if he had arrived moments earlier he could have stopped Jasim. If he had heard him inside their apartment, if he had recognized the threat, he could have stopped it. He knew who was at fault for Emy's death. He knew what he had to do.

TJ walked over to the kitchen and found the pistol he had kept hidden. Justice would be served. He would kill the man, the monster responsible for Emy's death. He was going to kill her killer.

Chapter Forty-Two

Emy woke up as TJ left the bed. She glanced at her phone and looked at a new alert. She checked her Facebook while waiting for TJ to return. She saw the living room light go on.

She remembered how worried TJ was about her and how threatened he felt. She stood and walked to the living room to make sure that TJ knew that she was okay.

When she entered the living room, she saw TJ raising a pistol to his head while his glazed eyes stared at the ground.

"NO!" she shrieked as she ran to him.

Chapter Forty-Three

TJ knew that no matter what happened or how he tried to explain it away, he was responsible for Emy's death. He hadn't killed Jasim when he had had the chance, nor did he stop Jasim when he followed him home. It was clear, it was he who was responsible for her death. TJ knew he deserved to die.

His finger was on the trigger as he raised the gun to his head.

He heard Emy scream. The sudden noise caused him to jerk and pull the trigger.

Emy watched her husband fall to the ground.

"No! No! No!" She screamed as blood began to seep from his head.

"Help!" she cried out as she attempted to cover the wound.

Moments later there was pounding on the door.

"Help us! Call 9-1-1!" she cried out. The door caved in, and their neighbor entered, phone in hand.

He called for an ambulance while doing his best to help Emy tend to TJ's wound.

Epilogue

Tucker took the paper from his superior.

"A new drug?" he thought to himself. *"Why does this pertain to me?"* He looked back to his superior.

"Why are you giving this to me?"

"You're getting a promotion. You will now be working hands-on with these drugs and the patients. It's an experimental drug protocol, so you'll need to report on how it is affecting those who take it.

"There is a chance that some will respond negatively, but that doesn't matter. Your job is to get the people to take the pills and continue to take them while you document how they react. Consistency is important. We feel we are on the verge of a major breakthrough, and we can't afford any bad information."

"Yes sir, I can do that. Just one question though, what kind of drug is it and how do I find the people that will be willing to take it?"

"It's a new type of anti-depressant. Twenty-two veterans commit suicide each day Tucker, and we can't afford that. This drug may be a gateway to ending PTSD once and for all."

"You will go to bases around the world and act as a mobile counselor to will establish connections. After that you can improvise, because officially, the State has no part in this.

"We need to know how this affects those who are in the field and not just those who are home and out for good.

"As you are aware, when someone is publicly suffering from this, we take him out of the field. Not this time. They stay active while you convince them you won't tell anyone about their "issues." Just make sure they get the pills continue to do their job, best they can."

"When do I start?"

"Tomorrow, you fly to Afghanistan. We have your first patient lined up. He has been kidnapped and is currently being tortured. We move in to rescue him tomorrow before you arrive. We will let the medics tend to his wounds, and then he's all yours."

"Sir, he is one of ours?"

"Yes."

"And he is being tortured, and we know where he is, but we aren't moving in to rescue him now?"

"Correct. Not acting immediately means there is a greater chance he will develop PTSD. We need to see how that medicine works. If this is how we speed up the progress of the program, then so be it. I will gladly let him suffer some if it means we can help many more a lot quicker."

"That sounds kind of callous, sir"

"It is. That's the way we have to be. You always need to be able and willing to do what is necessary to help the majority, even if it means a minority suffers. The number of veterans committing suicide it too much and we will bring that number down."

Tucker nodded his head and walked away clutching the small stack of papers that detailed what he would be doing.

Something didn't sit right with him. He was all for helping as many people as possible, but to do so at the expense of their own didn't feel right.

Tucker didn't like the idea, but he wasn't the one who was calling the shots. The one who did call the shots told Tucker he would be on a plane to Afghanistan to begin the drug trial, so that is what he would do.

"We need you to check up on some patients," his superior told him.

"Okay, when and where?"

"We have a plane ticket for you. You'll leave today and meet with TJ in Philadelphia. He'll be landing there and then heading back to Des Moines. You just need to meet him, talk with him briefly and make sure he's staying on the medicine.

"You will then leave Philadelphia and fly to Seattle. We have arranged for a few more of your patients to be there. We will give you more information when you arrive."

"Okay."

"I can't do it anymore." Tucker told his superior. "The price is already too high; I am not going to be responsible for this again. Ivan Lopez was a good man; this crap you're making me give these guys is what made this happen. I can't do it anymore. Lopez's blood is on my hands, along with the blood of his victims. I can't keep doing this. It is destroying people's lives. Look at what happened to TJ. I don't want any more blood on my hands. Look at John Noveske's research on drugs and this type of behavior."

"I understand your concern, but what you are doing is helping. We have already made vast advancements, at least, compared to what we would have otherwise."

"Look at his research!" Tucker yelled.

"Everything you are saying you don't like about this, we don't like either. We are working for the same outcome, but we have to take different angles. Your work is tremendously helpful. If you choose to stop now, then more will die before we can continue making progress. Everything you've done up to this point will be worthless. This isn't easy for anyone, but it's what is needed."

"But look at the damage it has already done," Tucker pleaded.

Made in the USA
Columbia, SC
25 June 2020

12075723R00121